THE THIRD THEME

Also by March Hastings

Abnormal Wife
Again and Again
The Boys of Brigham Dee
By Flesh Alone
Crack-Up
The Demands of the Flesh
Design for Debauchery
Enraptured
Fear of Incest
The Heat of the Day
Her Private Hell
The Jealous and Free
Obsessed
The Outcasts
A Rage Within
Savage Surrender
The Soft Way
Three Women
The Third Sex
The Third Theme
The Unashamed
Veil of Torment
Whip of Desire

THE THIRD THEME

MARCH HASTINGS

CUTTING EDGE

ISBN-13: 978-1-952138-85-0

Published by
Cutting Edge Books
PO Box 8212
Calabasas, CA 91372
www.cuttingedgebooks.com

CHAPTER ONE

"*Sharon... for chrissake, what're you doing in there?*"

Vaguely, she heard his voice. Its stab of anger forced open her heavy eyelids. Cool fingers of air stroked her naked skin and she shivered in the semidarkness.

The knob rattled. The wooden door shook in its warped frame.

"All right," she said from dry lips.

Her body turned in the silhouette of its perspiration and managed to sit up. She swallowed on a swollen throat and stared across the cluttered room at the crooked window shade sucked out to the fire escape. The weight of her dense black hair hung to her heavy breasts. She lifted each mass of flesh as though to free her body from its burden. A stale residue of salami and cigarette smoke wafted up from the fireplace litter. She sniffed and tried to remember if this were today or tomorrow or next week.

"I'm coming," she rasped with all her strength as the jiggling started again. Her feet met the carpeting and crinkled a scattering of manuscripts as she straightened toward equilibrium. "Coming..."

With a final effort at pride, she buttoned her trembling body into a housecoat and faltered toward the agony of facing him, like this, without any excuses.

The hugeness of him filled the doorway. In her numb dreams, she had forgotten the shock of his dark, glittering eyes, the bristle of his jaw. She sucked in a little breath and waited.

He stepped inside and slapped the door shut. "What is this?" he said without introduction.

His tweed jacket hung open. Beneath the tautness of the green polo shirt, she could see his rapid breathing. "You have no right..."

He grabbed her wrist and pulled her into the livingroom. With firm hands he set her back down on the couch. Then he strode to the window and let the shade up. He pulled the window wide. Moving in the last fragments of light, he swept up three small vials from bookcase, night table and television top.

"I don't get it," he said, standing in front of her now, his palm open, the sleeping pills clinking against plastic.

Sharon pressed her teeth tight together and waited some more. Waiting was what she knew how to do better than anything else in the world. Maybe, if she waited long enough, it would make sense to him that she wanted things the... normal way.

Somewhere above her, she heard him sigh. Disgust, probably. She closed her eyes and leaned forward. Her forehead touched the roughness of his jacket sleeve.

"No you don't."

His voice commanded her and she sat up rigid.

"Jay, stop yelling," she said in slow, tired words. And then her body began to yield, as it always did, to his presence. "Sit down." She patted the couch beside her.

The circulation of night air had started to waken all the lively nerves which had lain so drowsily. A tremor flickered along the inside of her thigh. "Please, darling." She gazed up the long, shadowed distance to his hard mouth.

"Please nothing." He pulled away, letting the vials drop and roll among the papers. "I've got a printer's schedule to meet. Bills to pay. High ones and lots of them."

She turned off the words and reached out to touch his thigh. Why was it so difficult for him to understand that she wasn't cut out to be editor of his silly magazines that could only talk about life but couldn't get down to the facts? For three years she had struggled to please him. To be the career girl he would have been proud of.

But it hadn't worked out. She understood now that it never would. Somewhere along the way, she had lost him.

Her fingers found the edge of his jacket. She tugged at one button, trying to pull him down beside her.

"Is that all you care about?" His icy words cut their way down to her.

Her shoulders hunched defensively. The tension prevented her from blurting useless words. How could she tell him of her plans? The bright, childish hope that had made her follow him to New York. What could he understand of her conventional need to be a wife for him, a mother to his children?

Giddy bubbles of futility floated in her head. The sleeping pills, the despair combined in a soft, careless laugh. Slowly, she stood up, rubbing herself along him as she moved. Her hands searched inside his jacket, caressing the muscles of his chest.

"Don't be an old sauerkraut," she heard her own lips say.

She flattened her hot breasts against the muscles of his ribs. In a single movement, she opened her housecoat, enfolding him within its yards of flowered material. What difference could it make that she despised herself?

"You bitch."

Roughly, his arms slid around her waist. She heard the flimsy material tear and felt it slither away. If only her body could be destroyed as easily, with so little pain.

Outside a congestion of deep throated trucks ground into gear and rolled up the bridge ramp. She remembered the smell of meat from the warehouses. Soon it would be summer again. The odor of death would be rising to greet her. How had she taken it for three years? Without complaint. Even light-heartedly.

Sharon lifted her hips and pressed her belly against the buckle of his belt. His face bruised along her throat, moving downward. Suddenly he lifted her and they were standing in the middle of the room. The breath huffed out of her as he pulled her tightly to him. She knew he liked it this way. As though they were standing in a train during rush hour. He liked so many things. So many women.

She heard the movement of his zipper and waited, helping him by lifting herself onto tiptoe. Her chin rested on his shoulder. She stared past into darkness. A breeze fluttered the papers. Now he didn't care about those manuscripts. Now they could go to hell. There were things more important to him, after all.

But she was not one of them.

Just himself.

Just his body. Just his needs, whatever they might be from one moment to another.

His elbows dug into her ribs and her thoughts went wild. She clung to his neck and pounded her body like surf against New England rock. The masses of her dark hair swung forward, covering his face.

Then in a sudden wave of convulsion, her knees gave way. So as not to fall, she hung on, her weight slipping along his legs, bending him with her to keep their contact.

Her teeth went into his shoulder. Then her mouth relaxed as the last quiver died along her ankles.

They were lying on the carpet among the manuscripts, the crusted glassware and all the other discarded pieces of her life. She blinked up at the ceiling to follow the outline of its sagging plaster.

"You know, Jay," she said, her fingertips massaging the back of his neck, "we've come a long way together."

"Mmm."

He rolled away from her and she heard him cracking his knuckles in that familiar action of impatience.

"I'm just sorry," she continued, "that all of it's been down." Her back tensed as she felt the pressure of the next sentence against her lips. She had not known until this instant what she was going to say. Or even that she was capable of saying it. "I'm quitting the job." Her voice was oddly calm. "And I'm quitting you."

With sudden, desperate energy, Sharon got up and rushed into the bathroom, locking the door until she heard his footsteps leave the apartment.

CHAPTER TWO

Silence pulsed around her. She snapped on the television set and flopped the channels over and over. Pictures zigzagged across her vision, reaching out hard enough to hit her, but not far enough to penetrate the loneliness.

Instinctively her hand groped for the telephone and brought it onto her lap. There were ten million people in New York City. Certainly one of them would be glad to spend the night with her. A party, a movie, a dance, a bottle. She didn't much care which. Or with whom.

Memories of faces swung through her thoughts. Men whom she had never gotten to know well because of Jay.

Now she could make up for lost time.

She chose the blond, soft spoken Kermit Drake who had seemed to her then particularly dangerous.

Sharon leafed through her address book and found his number. They had hashed over his manuscripts often enough so that she felt almost natural, calling him now.

When his low voice drawled hello, Sharon felt a light sigh of relief waft through her. Let happen what might tomorrow. Tonight, at least, she would not have to be alone.

Yes, he had a party and yes, he was surprised to hear from her but wasn't it about time she got back among the living? Sure he'd be glad to meet her uptown or just as happy to come call, if she'd rather. No? Then Sixty-Ninth Street would be best. Corner of Lex . . .

Good boy, Kermit, she thought, dropping the receiver back. Never the wrong questions...

Sharon lowered herself into the tub of hot water and leaned slowly back to rest her head against the porcelain. Closing her eyes, she gave herself to the warmth, feeling it lap along the sides of her breasts, letting it float her arms and draw out the knotted tensions. Tonight she would sparkle. Tonight she would come alive again. Out of the oyster shell at last. Free to follow her inclinations. Free to give of herself to the whole world.

Despite a twinge of fear, Sharon felt a delicious shiver. What was it going to be like, this new freedom? What were all the things she really wanted to do? A little smile forced its way to her lips, anticipating the pleasures of discovery.

Sharon towelled herself with brisk motions, whipping higher the glow of adventure. A touch of perfume to the backs of her thighs, her shoulders, and in the wisps of hair at her neck. Fresh violet-hued lipstick that made her hazel eyes a round, catlike yellow. Then she rummaged through the storage closet and found the Spring dress she'd had made to celebrate Jay's birthday. She pulled closed its long zipper over the contour of her spine and swirled the whispering satin material around her hips. A pity Jay would never see it on her.

But Kermit would appreciate her just as well. Probably better. No strings attached. Only fun. Kermit, she felt instinctively, would be lots of fun when tapped on his non-professional levels. Too bad he wrote for Taft Publications. No doubt he would let slip to Jay something about tonight. Too bad? Sharon thought about it again and realized what a distinct satisfaction it would be to have Jay discover she'd gone out on the very night of their separation.

She agreed with herself enthusiastically and yet, at the same time, a cavern of depression opened hollowly in the center of her stomach. Slipping into her velvet pumps, she got out a dusty bottle of brandy and swallowed a mouthful. It occurred to Sharon that she had not eaten in two days. No wonder her legs felt trembly.

With surging need to escape from the apartment, she flung on a velvet coat and clattered down the dirty stairway into a cool, star-sprayed night.

A huddle of kids giggled in the shadow of a car fender. Others wisecracked in the yellow beam of a lamppost. Life vibrated around Sharon as her metal heels clicked smartly, taking her to the intersection where she hailed a cab.

At her command, the car swerved and hurtled through traffic. Sharon leaned back and watched the mingling of people, automobiles and store lights slide past. The world, it seemed, had rallied to her defense tonight.

As the cab slowed, Sharon spotted the lanky outline of his navy suit. She reached forward to pay, then stepped quickly to the curb without waiting for change.

"Hi," she said, coming up behind him and linking her arm through his. She felt his body turn slightly, with slow calm.

His blue-green gaze seemed to engulf her. "Hi, yourself," he said.

A tremor of pleasure made her unsteady. The charming manner she had wanted to use seemed to spill and roll in a thousand directions out of her reach. "Am I too early?"

"Not at all." A gentle smile spread along the narrow length of his smooth face. The breeze flicked up a single strand of his blond hair so carefully brushed along his temples. "Any time with you is fine with me."

His manner stroked down the ruffles of her nerves. Easily, Sharon returned his smile. He seemed, somehow, so harmless, so anxious to please. And yet she could feel the lurking masculinity, waiting, watching.

They began to stroll crosstown, away from the weekend crowds. Gradually the tall buildings with their doormen and canopies were replaced by rows of self-effacing brownstones.

"Maybe you know Ralph and Leda Michaels?" he said. "That's where we're going."

"No. Should I?" Sharon felt an instant's prickle of irritation as she thought of Jay. She almost said that it was a miracle she knew anyone at all.

Kermit shrugged. "He's a writer. I thought all editors knew all writers."

Sharon caught the tone of mock innocence and wondered if there were anything special about this Ralph Michaels. It would have to be something sordid to account for the special casualness of Kermit's question.

"They're nice people," Kermit continued, filling in the silence.

"I'm sure."

The need to do something immense to forget Jay, to abandon herself was spreading through Sharon like wild wine. Purposely, she leaned against Kermit's arm. Through his wool jacket, she could feel the outline of muscle. Its solidity reassured her.

"You're going to have a good time tonight," he said.

"Of course I am," Sharon murmured. Ever so slightly, she squeezed his arm. Obviously he knew why she was here tonight. He would have been a fool not to. And he was willing to help her. "We're both going to have a wonderful time," she added with energy.

If she could only chuck the odd, unfamiliar wispiness that was making her body feel lighter than air. The moment they got inside, she must make sure to eat something. That's what it was, certainly. The brandy on her empty stomach. And it must have been the drink, too, that seemed to be clogging up her hearing. All of her felt like an inflated ball of cotton, tumbling along beside him. *Kermit,* she wanted to say, *Kermit, take care of me.*

"This is it," he said at last, stopping at the end of a tree-lined street.

She followed him past a black painted gate and down three steps to a black door with a large brass knocker.

"It's only for show," Kermit grinned as he pressed a button.

The whole place seemed only for show, Sharon decided as a green-uniformed maid led them across black and white marble into the smoke and din of a tremendous livingroom.

Some heads turned as they entered but no one came to greet them.

"Are you sure we're invited?" Sharon said with a slight edge of acid in her voice.

Kermit's hand slipped to her waist and steered her around Martini glasses and cigarette holders. "You know how these things are," he said.

But as she clung to him, her glance moved curiously over some of the other women. In the pale red lighting, their faces seemed grotesque. Some were straining with sophisticated laughter, others wide-eyed in feigned admiration of male talk, still others aloof in cool silence. All of them half gone with alcohol.

Involuntarily she moved closer to Kermit. "Can we manage something to eat?" she said, tilting her face to his ear. She must remember to stay very, very sober.

"Sure thing."

He brought her past a group of three men in sun glasses and deep tans.

"What'll it be?"

She stood in front of the long array of small sandwiches and mounds of chopped and mashed foods. "Anything," she said. "But pile it high."

She could feel the dozens of strange people behind her back. And as Sharon ate, her desire to mingle with them began to stir. She wanted to peer, to pry, to understand and share. Mingle her destiny, become absorbed, forget her own story for awhile.

While she ate, Kermit stood beside her, sipping straight whiskey from a highball glass. "How about something like this for you?"

"Not just yet, thanks."

"Don't tell me you're the sober type?"

"Hardly."

They laughed, softly, with that subtle flow of intimacy she'd felt before. He lit two cigarettes and handed her one.

"This isn't what you'd call the friendliest party in the world," she said, needing to keep their conversation alive. If she talked long enough, laughed long enough, made love to enough people, it would bury other feelings that floated just beneath the surface.

"Oh, friendly enough," he said. "You just haven't noticed."

The food began to settle in her stomach and her legs were becoming steadier. All she had to do now was wait. If she waited only another minute, she'd be part of all this, not just watching.

"Ralph is somewhere in this mess," he continued. "But you don't want me to go looking for him."

"Of course not," Sharon answered, to be obliging.

Slowly, she began to examine the faces with more care. And she noticed that glances did dart occasionally back at her. A few times her gaze ran smack up against a smile. And she smiled back, hoping the man or woman would come over to join them. She had no intention of standing here at the buffet all evening, watching Kermit get drunk.

She watched him fill his third glass, then another, and bring them over.

"How about it?" he said, offering one.

"All right." Sharon took the glass and held it without drinking. She could toy with it the rest of the night. Nurse it along. Even ask for another when the ice cubes melted. But no drinking. Even the thought of drinking sent shivers along the insides of her arms.

And with the shivers came the burst of loneliness that she had been sitting on all this while. She leaned over very close and rested one palm on his lapel. "Talk to me," she said.

"And what would you like me to talk to you about?"

She watched the movement of his lips. They were soft, very red lips. The whole face was so smooth, unscarred by razor nicks, clean. The green eyes had grown larger, it seemed, their lashes making a fan shaped shadow. Almost a girl's face, she thought. Nothing brutal, nothing selfish. His gaze seemed to be reaching out to encircle her, to hold her like a child. To comfort. To help forget. He put his hand lightly on her shoulder. His forefinger touched her neck.

"Just talk to me, Kermit," she pleaded. "About anything."

"Okay," he said slowly. "I'll tell you about the rabbits."

She listened to the rise and ebb of his voice; making a design of words for her pleasure. As he talked, she moved still closer, wanting to feel the warmth of his arms around her, the reassuring touch of flesh, the knowledge of a heartbeat.

She was about to lean her cheek against his shoulder.

"And here's Kerm Drake," a man's voice said with a shock of amused surprise.

Instead of her cheek, a broad, heavy hand came down with a slap on Kermit's shoulder.

"What the hell are you doing at one of my brawls?" Tumbles of curly brown hair fell forward to cover the deepening wrinkles of a high forehead.

"Same as you," Kermit said. "Trying to enjoy myself."

The stocky man in the flowered shirt turned now and peered at Sharon. "And who's the gorgeous doll?"

Kermit seemed to insinuate his shoulder in a way that prevented the man from reaching out to touch her. "An old, old friend," he said. "Not to be damaged by window shoppers."

"Come, come now." The voice was a little high, a little too carefree. "What have I ever damaged?"

"Sharon Porter, this is our sozzled old host, and I'm surprised that the two of you haven't ever done business together." He took Sharon's hand, connected it for a quick hand shake with Ralph's, and separated them again.

"But I'd love to do business with the lady," Ralph's voice squeaked from a reddening face. "It was you who said I couldn't."

"No, we've never met," Sharon put in quickly. Sooner or later, she would have to go into a full confession. Tell Kermit that she had quit the job. Tell him that she intended to leave New York on Monday or as soon as she could sublet the apartment.

"Tell you what, doll. When this hunk of taffy folds over his glass, you come lookin' for me, will you? I'll be right … over … there," he said, pointing toward the ceiling. "And," he turned to Kermit, "if you should happen to run into my wife in your travels around this pig pen, tell her I've come home for tea, will you?"

As he toddled away on stiff legs, Kermit said, "So now that you've met the host?"

"I'd be curious to meet the hostess," Sharon said thoughtfully.

"Oh, would you now?"

"Yes."

"Why?"

"Oh, I don't know. I get strange emanations." Sharon turned the glass in her hand and watched the ice cubes bob. Meeting Ralph had brought out a film of sweat along her back. She had looked into his eyes and seen the reflection of her own despair. But it was a despair that had grown cynical with age. Would it happen to her? Would she too wander through life, helpless and puzzled?

Impulsively, the glass moved to Sharon's lips. She took a quick hard swallow. "I don't want to stand around," she said. "Dance with me."

"Without music?"

Her lips tilted in a challenging smirk and her eyelids half closed. "Since when does an operator like you need music?" She lifted her arms and moved her hips in close to him. She felt his arms against her back. Her spine curved with the pressure.

"Anything the lady says."

She put her cheek against his striped tie and inhaled the odor of soap that emanated from his crisp white shirt. They stood together beside the table, swaying in place. She felt the crowd and the sadness beginning to close in.

"At a shindig like this," she said, "there ought to be entertainment."

"We make our own."

She felt his lips touch her ear.

"Tell me about it," she said.

"It's not the kind of thing that lends easily to talk."

"But you'll be glad to show me?"

"You know it."

"Get me another drink," she said, handing him the empty glass.

"My pleasure."

As he disappeared among the crowd, Sharon moved away from the table. She did not want to be stuck here at one end of the long room. There was so much going on. So much she would be missing. So many opportunities to meet people. Men who would take over where Kermit left off. A never-ending line of men who wouldn't let her be alone with herself for a single instant.

All she had to do was let the room know that she was accessible.

She felt a sudden desire to tap everyone on the shoulder and introduce herself. You could do things like that at a party.

"Hey, I almost lost you." Kermit caught up with her and put the drink into her hand.

"I was just going to make us some friends," she said and grinned innocently at the disappointment on his face that lifted one blond eyebrow.

"But I thought we were self-sufficient."

"We are, darling, we are," Sharon said quickly, not wanting to hurt him.

"The trouble is," he said, "that this crowd is making you dizzy. Come on, I'll take you where it's private and tell you the story of my life."

"But I like crowds," she protested, taking a fast swallow of her drink and then another. "In fact, I love crowds."

"And me?"

"Oh, I love you, most of all." Her voice came out in a giddy laugh.

Sharon felt a twinge of discomfort creeping up from her ankles. As though she had been keeping count of something that insisted on going by too fast.

"Then come with me."

She had started this game between them. And now Sharon responded to the challenge in his low words with a genial nod. Why not? Why not let impulse carry her to unexpected adventures? Wasn't this what she had promised herself? Wasn't this what she had been missing all these years? And wasn't Kermit the one she had chosen to help her break through the glass walls that imprisoned her from Life ... whatever Life might be?

"Kermit," she slid her hand into his pocket and massaged his hip bone through the material. "Kermit, I give you credit for lots of imagination."

He put his hand in over hers and squeezed her fingers gently.

They moved around the edge of the room, passing alongside the green velvet drapes that camouflaged windows and walls. "You see," he chatted at random, "article writers have an inventive attitude toward living. They can't help it."

"I hope that includes your friend Ralph."

"You seem to have him on the brain, don't you?"

Sharon overlooked the mild curiosity in his voice. They had reached the entrance hall and he led her back across the marble flooring to a wide staircase.

"Not that I blame you," Kermit continued. "He's rich, always at loose ends, and very susceptible to young, hungry women."

"Like me," she said flatly, taking the carpeted steps lightly. "Like you."

"But, of course, that's not the whole truth of it at all," Sharon said, letting her fingertips trail along the wide mahogany bannister.

"That you're hungry?"

"No. That Ralph's susceptible."

They reached the first landing marked off by a hallway lined with odd-shaped modern paintings.

"But he is."

"Nope," Sharon insisted. "He might pretend to be."

"And you? Are you pretending, too?"

They stood facing each other very close and she saw the movement of his tongue.

"I wish I were," Sharon breathed with more sincerity than she had intended. The two drinks had begun to slacken the taut reins of her propriety. She leaned against the bannister and waited for her breathing to slow. Something inside her felt the need to rush headlong into ... Into what? She didn't know, couldn't see the destiny toward which her body yearned. But she could feel still the shadow of Jay, touching, poisoning her freedom. For an instant, she felt like a monkey on the end of a long rope. She could run and tumble and play around ... so long as she did not try to run too far.

"You know what I think," Kermit said, as his fingers inched along her ribs. "I think you're trying very hard to feel sorry for yourself."

"Perhaps." She did not try to stop his hands. Instead, she leaned in closer. "But why do you say it?"

"Because you're too damned eager."

Sharon stiffened.

"You're playing it like a starving urchin at the country fair." His hands tightened around her waist. "Someone would think I was about to kiss a virgin."

His lips came down on hers quick and hard, drowning the tumble of protesting words rising to her throat. She felt the curves of his leanness, the unexpected hardness of his chest, the squeezing pressure of his biceps. Then he stood back from her just as quickly.

"Think, maybe, you can relax soon and enjoy yourself?"

"But I am," she said. "I'm enjoying myself more than you know." Her words sounded bitten off, hard as a spinster's bitterness. She had wanted him to be good to her, to help her forget herself in a stream of lovely lies. A cold stab of disappointment slit her in half as she realized the necessity of defending herself from Kermit, too.

"Maybe you just can't enjoy something that doesn't come hard," she said.

"Maybe. But if you're so damn easy, I'd like to know what's coming next."

"You're writing this story," she said. "Why don't you just play it by ear?" She motioned for him to give her another cigarette. "And besides, who ever heard of a woman having to do the coaxing?"

"Oh, lady, you don't scare me off with all this phony contempt. You only reinforce my original theory that you're not really as ready-for-anything as you'd like me to believe."

Sharon let the cigarette dangle from the center of her lips. "But you haven't tested me yet."

She had backed herself into a corner. Obviously Kermit was more aware than she had realized. Aware of her wild need to throw herself at people. "I'm not out to play the clinging vine," she said. "You don't have to worry."

They had begun to climb up the second flight. All sounds of the party were drowned away. She could hear only the soft sliding of their shoes on the nap of the rug.

"I understand that," he said. "But frankly, I don't think you know what you're out to do."

"Oh, yes I do," she said on the crest of a low, angry laugh.
"Well?"

But Sharon paused. What good would it do to tell him of
her ambition to dissolve the past and create a whole new future?
There was nothing so definite in her scheme that she could tell
him something that made practical sense. And what business
was it of Kermit's anyway? He was here to supply her with a good
time, not to make like the Wise Old Owl.

"My sole purpose tonight," she said, "is to have a swinging
ball. And that's why I called you in on the scene."

"Nonsense."

"So don't believe me."

"Don't worry, I don't."

It felt strangely awkward, fighting with him like this, so suddenly, in the middle of nowhere, when she was out to do everything humanly possible to please the man.

Sharon paused in the middle of the steps. "Why are we arguing?" she said.

"It's simple. I don't like to be used." He grinned. "I want to be
loved for myself."

She felt her cheeks go cold. "I didn't think of it that way," she
said.

"Most women don't."

"And there's no denying it," she went on. "I did call you up to
help take my mind off Jay. But I thought you knew that."

"Sure I knew it."

"Then I don't understand."

He took the stub of her cigarette and pressed it out on the
bottom of his shoe. "Well, I expected by now that you'd square
with me about the whole situation. I'm not the kind of guy
who's in the habit of playing nursemaid without any kind of
explanation."

"Nursemaid." Sharon felt an impulse to turn and run down
the stairs, out of the house.

"Wait a minute," Kermit said before she could move. "I didn't mean to fight with you."

"But you're right," she said, "and I can't bear to face myself. I wanted you to play with me, distract me. And that certainly wasn't very fair to you."

He moved down a step and touched her hair. "Well, let's see if we can't work out something more mutually beneficial."

Sharon's guilt subsided into a docile desire to give of herself more sincerely. It wasn't her intention to turn into a prize bitch just because one man had made a fool of her.

"Where are we going?" she said, in an effort to change the subject.

"In here," he said, pushing open a panelled door. "This is the music room. You said you like music."

Shelves of records lined one wall to the ceiling. A baby grand piano stood in one corner, a sectional couch diagonally opposite. Except for a low table with cigarettes and a bottle of Scotch, there was no other furniture.

The lighting came from behind the couch in a soft, spreading glow. Sharon went to the couch, lowered herself onto the foam rubber and put up her feet.

"Have they got any jazz from Paris?" she said.

"Let's look."

She closed her eyes and began wiggling her shoes off. They fell to the mustard colored rug and toppled over. Reaching to the table, she lifted a cigarette and rolled it between her fingers, not wanting to smoke, not wanting to do anything that required conscious effort. She heard him move the arm of a record player and then the rhythmic chords began in open clusters of tone calculated to drug her senses.

"Lower," she said, and he turned down the volume. Her body stretched inside the confines of her girdle. She spread her legs and felt the elastic tight against her thighs. "Come here, Kermit," she said, her voice part of the music.

She felt him standing beside her. Felt the light stream of his breathing.

"Undress me," she said without opening her eyes.

She heard the movement of his clothing as he knelt. His fingers crept slowly up underneath the hem of her dress. She felt them fumbling with the garters, releasing the tension of her stockings. Then he slid them down along her thighs, moving along her calves, her ankles.

"Your feet are cold," he said, his voice hardly above a whisper.

Sharon smiled. "Really?"

"Cold feet, warm heart." He dropped the second stocking on top of the first one.

"I thought it was cold hands."

"You say it your way."

Sharon turned onto her side, pressing the tip of her nose to the tufts of the couch back. "That's a long, difficult zipper," she said. "Be careful, it sticks."

She stretched one arm above her head, leaning backward to make it easier.

"Good little zipper," he said.

She felt a triangle of air touch her naked back. Then his lips moving along the rim of her bra. A moment later the single hook came open. The weight of her breasts sagged freely.

One of his hands came along the side of her breast and cupped around the nipple, playing slowly till she sensed the tip of it harden. Her thoughts began to sway in a slow circle.

"Kermit," she said, "are you drunk?"

"No." His lips moved along her arm.

"I think I am."

No answer.

"Do you care if I'm drunk, Kermit?" She fell again onto her back and brought his face up very close to her own.

"No, I don't care," he said.

Sharon smiled and ran her tongue along the outline of his lips. "Good. You know why? Because I'm going to get even drunker."

She struggled to sit up. The front of her dress slithered down over the brassiere from which her breasts had escaped. "This silly thing," she laughed, tugging at the brassiere. "It thinks it's a necklace."

Reaching across to the table, she got the bottle and sat it down on her knees.

"Here, I'll get it open for you."

She waited while he uncorked it.

"No glasses," he said.

"So?" She took the bottle back from him and lifted it to her lips.

It ran down her throat in swallows of liquid desire. She had always known this about herself. A predisposition that ran through her family. Two drinks and all the sex spigots turned on. Full. She had first given herself to Jay after a few drinks. Raped him was closer to the truth.

Her fingers moved crablike to find contact with Kermit. Her hand landed on his knee and began to explore.

"How about sharing that bottle?" he said.

She had already swallowed enough to last her all week. "Be my guest," she said, pushing it toward him across his lap.

Kermit set it on the table without drinking.

"You cheater," Sharon muttered.

"I won't cheat you," he said from against her throat. "Damn well better not."

The insistence of music was seeping in through her flesh. She kicked away her dress and began to claw at the hooks of her girdle. "Open, damn you, open."

"Come on, let me have a try," he said gently.

"Tear it, if necessary," she said from grim, tight lips.

"It won't be."

She felt the series of hooks coming undone one after the other. Her flesh began to expand with the relief of her body's freedom.

"Why do women wear these things anyway?" he said. "Especially ones with figures like yours?"

"Upbringing." She laughed on a sudden, shrill note. "Didn't you know all mothers teach their little girls that it isn't ladylike to go around with their behinds jiggling?"

"You've got a lovely..."

Her fingers went into his hair and brought his lips in reach of her mouth. "I don't want to talk any more."

She lifted herself toward him, arching upward, seeking the body and soul of him beneath his clothes. Hastily she pulled out his shirttail and found the warm outlines of muscle over his ribs and upward along his back. He felt smooth. Almost hairless. Smooth as a girl, she thought again. Not like Jay.

The vision of Jay exploded across the dark background of her closed eyelids. She squinted and buried her face beneath his chin, pressing herself upward, twining her limbs around the long body to become one with him.

She felt the drive of his desire meeting her own, whipping the flames of her craving, higher, faster.

They fell halfway off the couch when it happened. She slid down the rest of the way, pulling him with her.

They were lying under the table when Sharon came awake to the world. The carpet was cleaner, the room larger, the atmosphere more exclusive than it had been with Jay. But she was still on the floor looking up.

Sharon sighed and a knot of tears came to her throat.

CHAPTER THREE

Sharon took her time getting dressed. What was there to hurry for? The future, the glorious future which had promised to rush at her seemed like a dirty trick, an April Fool's joke.

"Turn off that lousy noise," she muttered. "It's beating the sides of my head in."

She turned away from the sight of him going naked across the room. The rims of her lids grated on her eyeballs. Her stomach sloshed and her temples thudded.

"Better?" he said.

She plunged into the room's sudden silence. "How good can it be," she said, "when you're sober?"

She felt herself being lifted from the floor. Dragged up by her armpits and sat down on the couch.

"We ought to try getting dressed," he said.

"Why? Are they waiting in line for this room?"

She had no reason to be nasty to him. She didn't even feel nasty. "I'm sorry," she said, a little more clearly. "Alcohol tears me apart."

"We can get you aspirin, once you're dressed."

"No. I've got to chuck it up. That's the only thing that helps."

"There's a john down the hall." He spoke while he gathered the various pieces of her underwear scattered around the floor.

Sharon squinted at the wreckage of her clothing. "How am I ever going to get back into all that?"

"Just try," he said. "I'll help you."

Painfully she began stuffing her bloated torso into the elastic that now mysteriously refused to stretch.

"I just can't," she sighed and folding it into a tiny square, pushed the girdle beneath the sofa pillow.

Somehow she got her dress on over just bra and panties, wriggled barefoot into her shoes and patted down the tumble of her hair.

"To your left," Kermit said and pointed her along the hall. "Second door from the end."

Sharon stumbled down the corridor, fighting to control herself from passing out.

She turned on the cold water tap full force and lowered her head to spatter her face. With a sudden burst, her guts seemed to come up and then she stood tired and panting, but released from the misery. She sat down on the edge of the tub and waited for strength to return. For all she cared, she might as well sit here in this bathroom until Monday. Obviously there was no hope for her in a large city. She couldn't take care of herself. And there was no one here interested enough to take on the responsibility for her survival. She couldn't blame Kermit for letting her down all that alcohol. She could only blame herself for being stupid and childish and desperate enough to fool herself into believing that she could escape the misery of Jay's betrayal.

No, there was no way out for her. No simple, secure, safe way to slide into maturity. She would simply have to go back to Lynbrook, pick up the scattered pieces of her life and begin all over again.

She stood up and opened the mirrored door of the medicine cabinet above the sink. In it, she found a variety of combs and lipsticks which no doubt belonged to Ralph's wife. But there was no stomach settler or headache pills or other medication. A healthy family, she thought. But Ralph hadn't looked so healthy.

With a heavy hand, she began to fix her appearance. In the direct bathroom light, she could see harsh lines of fatigue around her mouth and dark smudges of tension beneath her eyes. She looked used. Used up. And it was no surprise. She could just imagine the comments from friends and family back home. Not the open comments to her face. But the one behind her back. It wasn't going to be exactly easy back home, either.

But that was Monday and this was only Friday night. Slowly, she took the pins out of her straggled hair and began to roll another chignon. Two whole days to live through. Daytime wouldn't be too bad, though. It was just the nights and the darkness. If she could manage to keep Kermit with her until dawn, she would be all right.

As she thought this, Sharon knew it would be difficult. He had urged her to dress, anxious to get rid of her and the gloom that she spread. She looked at her ashen face and realized that it didn't exactly give off the mood of a good time Charlie.

She heard a gentle knock at the door and turned off the water. "I'll be right out, Kermit," she said with artificial good spirits. "I'm feeling much better now."

Swiftly, she rouged her cheeks and fixed a luminous smile in her eyes. Then she flung open the door and emerged in a grand sweep of enthusiasm.

But it wasn't Kermit who stood waiting.

Sharon found herself looking into golden brown eyes smiling with amusement.

"No one's mistaken me for Kerm in ages," the woman said.

She stood exactly Sharon's height and her smile seemed close enough to touch. Her silver blonde hair covered a small head with curls like a young boy out of ancient Greece. Sharon couldn't tell how old she was.

"Where is he, anyhow?" she continued in a velvet voice. "I haven't seen the man in much too long."

"The music room." Sharon barely managed to keep herself from stuttering. "I left him in there."

"Is it a good party?" the woman said as they walked together. "I haven't been downstairs yet."

"Very crowded."

"Good. Then no one will miss me."

"Ralph did, hours ago," Sharon said impulsively.

"Do I look that much married?" As she turned her head, a small gold earring gleamed from one lobe. The white turtle neck blouse and single piece jumper combined to hide the shape of her. Only a subtle curve of firm breast and long waistline revealed the slimness beneath.

Unable to answer the question without embarrassment, Sharon introduced herself instead. And she tried to walk slowly, hoping that Kermit would be dressed by the time they reached the room.

But inevitably, they arrived at the door. Holding a deep breath, Sharon pushed it open.

"That's better," Kermit said, fixing in place the second cuf-flink. "Well, look who you caught."

Sharon remained discreetly in the background while the two friends greeted each other. She noticed that the woman wore san-dals and was therefore much taller than she had realized. And she noticed too the tan on her naked legs, the freedom of her movements with Kermit. With a twinge of annoyance, Sharon wondered if these two had ever slept together.

"Now this is going to be a real party," Kermit said, moving Leda down to the couch.

"No, I can't stay, really. But why don't you two come down-stairs with me?"

"Leda, please." Kermit found a pipe in the inside pocket of his jacket. "Not that melee."

"But I've got to, you know that. Look, I've delayed as long as I could. It must be midnight by now. Just an hour?"

Sharon realized that the woman was looking directly at her. "I don't mind," she answered. Somehow, it didn't make any dif-ference whether Kermit liked the idea or not.

"Good."

The three of them proceeded downstairs.

"You know, if it were up to me," Leda said, "I'd move out every Friday night."

"I don't believe you," Kermit said. "You enjoy these massacres even more than Ralph does."

"Do I?"

"Yes. Otherwise you wouldn't permit it."

Sharon listened to the banter, trying to understand the quality of the woman's charm. Obviously Kermit, too, was very impressed with her. He spoke in a more polished, careful manner, seemingly trying to impress her, though they were old friends.

When they reached the living room, she felt the touch of Leda's palm on her elbow.

"I don't want you to get lost."

The whispered words startled Sharon. But she felt no desire to object. If anything, she was glad for the attention being paid to her. She needed something more to do, now that Kermit was finished with her. She had a person to wonder about; a person who, it seemed, was wondering about her. Sharon knew she could drag the little game out for the rest of the night. And maybe through some of tomorrow. Leda was a good time killer and therefore heaven sent.

Sharon followed along Leda's path of introductions. Some of the names she had dealt with through the mails, some she had heard of from other parts of the entertainment world. But they were simply people like herself, anxious to escape their own thoughts, anxious to delay facing their own lives, wasters.

And always there remained to haunt her the question of how Leda fitted into this group, what she enjoyed about it . . .

"Nothing more to drink, thank you," Sharon said with excessive patience as Kermit brought over three glasses.

"Let the child be," Leda interjected as Kermit started to object. "This isn't a booze hall."

For no reason that she could name, Sharon felt the strain seeping out of the muscles along her neck. She knew that Leda would keep her occupied for quite some time to come.

Although she remained stark sober, Sharon felt herself drifting on a fury-driven tide of nonchalance.

Leda obligingly introduced her to everyone they passed. Some Sharon met for the second and third time. Others had just arrived. As the hours progressed, the party seemed to be blossoming around her.

"There are more people here tonight," she said, accepting a glass of plain ginger ale, "than in my home town."

Kermit rested his elbow on the back of a high wooden chair. "Good thing you left."

"You sound nostalgic," Leda said, as a young bearded boy kissed her cheek in passing.

"Sharon thinks people in home towns are pure, altruistic and desirous of marrying her off to an ambitious, lovable chap with whom she will be happy forever."

"So did I, ten years ago," Leda put in and covered Sharon's flushed expression. "And the town gave me Ralph."

"I didn't know Ralph was ambitious."

"And I didn't know you, my sweet Kermit, were such a louse."

Sharon listened to their banter, feeling herself out of it. Their talk glittered to her as party baubles ought to glitter. And yet it seemed calculated for her own particular amusement. The spoiling of a cranky child.

As she sensed this, Sharon warmed and expanded. Her smile and approval stretched greedily for more. Jay had never spoiled her. Jay had never given a thought to what she might need or want. After all the years of giving to him, she felt a hollow place in her gaping wide with unsated desires. She had given of herself so freely in the past: now she intended to take with the same freedom of selfishness she had seen in others.

This bright resolve stirred in Sharon vaguely, without words. She felt it in the passiveness of her flesh, the expectant interest as she watched Leda.

"How about a chair for the aching bones?" Leda said and began to turn around the one on which Kermit was leaning.

Kermit's hand gripped the chair in place. "No, don't make her too comfortable. We have to be leaving soon."

"So early?" Sharon said, allowing disappointment to pout on her mouth.

"Early? Honey, it's after four." He reached to take her glass. "There's always a Leda party. You'll be back, I guarantee."

Sharon moved her glass out of reach. "But I like this one."

Kermit paused uncertainly. He blinked down at Sharon. She could feel the stirring of anger as his eyes darkened.

"And I think I will sit down," she said lightly. "Thank you, Leda."

Kermit's mouth tightened. He pulled out the cigarette case, flicked it open and saw there were no cigarettes inside. It snapped shut loudly.

"All right, Kerm, supposing you go get your sleep and Ralph and I will see to your friend."

Sharon's pout switched to a broad smile. "I don't mind."

"No, I'll bet you don't," he said thoughtfully. "All right. Good night." He turned on the clipped words and began pushing his way to the door.

They watched him till he reached the doorway.

"Sometimes men are such babies," Sharon said on the breath of a sigh.

"The two of you seemed friendly enough earlier."

"Oh, we're friendly. I simply don't know him very well. I certainly didn't know he was subject to such moods." As Sharon emphasized the last word, she tilted her head up toward Leda. "Women are so much more stable, aren't they?"

Leda's head went back on the curve of a laugh that seemed to shake the whole of her supple body. "I wouldn't vouch for that at all."

Sharon felt the leather chair molded comfortably to her back. An echo of satisfaction murmured pleasantly through her, now that Kermit was gone. She wouldn't have to humor Leda. Put up with any stuffy superiority. She could feel that Leda wanted to please her. And if the woman wanted to do things for her, why not?

Sharon tried pounding exuberance into herself, yet it felt like the pummeling of a straw filled sack. She could not really ignore the nervous aching in her calves, the worn, drained feeling in her stomach, the soreness beginning to develop in her throat. The skin of her cheeks felt like a dry mask. To smile even a little required mountainous effort.

But she dared not seek a bed or sleep. Sleep meant dreams beyond her control. And lack of control meant ... No, she dared not even think about it here, in this crowded room, with this attentive woman so eager to help.

"You're miles away from here, aren't you?"

Leda's voice cut through her thoughts. "No, I'm right here," she lied hurriedly. "Right here with you and all this fun."

"Just listen to that voice," Leda's hand patted her head. "How would you like to come back into the kitchen where we can get some nice hot coffee?"

Sharon searched the woman's face and found only kindliness in the soft eyes.

"Yes," she said simply and swallowed the wave of protest that had risen automatically to defend her falsehood.

They went down half a flight and across a linoleum corridor into a long kitchen. It was the first room from which Sharon could see out the windows.

The empty streets stretched in the cold, desolate lull before dawn. Endless lonely silence seemed to reach in, wanting to drag

Sharon into itself. She sat down at a narrow table along the wall and turned her back to the windows.

Yet the sense of time and recognition of the waiting day jostled the brittle mood of gaiety.

"Tell me about yourself," she said quickly, needing to fill her mind with thoughts that didn't matter. "Tell me how it feels to be rich."

Leda stood at the birch cupboard, spooning coffee into a percolator. "Lousy, if you must know," she said while she adjusted the flame. "Sometimes, when I'm feeling really low, I kid myself that if I had given away this house and the bonds and the bank accounts, Ralph and I would have stood a chance. Then the sensible mood arrives and I'm thankful to be able to afford private schools for the kids." She lifted broken pieces of a glass from the steel sink and dropped them into a steel container. "Yeah, we have a boy eight and Tony is five. I just cross my fingers that they'll grow up like neither one of us."

Sharon crossed her legs and pressed her thighs together, trying to squeeze away a growing depression. She hadn't expected to hear troubles. Leda didn't seem like the kind of woman to have domestic problems. For some stupid reason, she had assumed that Leda had Ralph under control and the world under her thumb.

"Isn't there anyone around without hard luck?" she said without covering the annoyance she felt in her disillusion.

"Don't call it hard luck," Leda smiled. "That makes it sound almost unbearable." She set out cups and napkins. "And unbearable makes me think of Ralph again, which isn't very nice on a lovely weekend night."

"Then why don't you divorce him?"

"And lose custody of the kids? My little friend, I would blush to tell you the stories that man would not hesitate to bring to court if I challenged his position as head of this household."

In counterpoint, the coffee began to perk in merry plops, bringing a sunny morning atmosphere to the placid hopelessness of their conversation.

Sharon rolled the edge of her napkin, making a long cylinder. "I thought everybody could run away," she said.

"Everybody? I never met anyone who could," Leda spoke from behind a closet door and brought out boxes of cookies.

"Here's one," Sharon said on an impulse to demonstrate the possibility of her point. "I'm going to run away from everything that's dragged me down and start all over again. You don't believe it?"

"I wish you luck."

"Why don't you believe it?" Sharon insisted. "I'm young. There's a whole new life waiting for me someplace."

"You make it sound like retiring to Florida on a pension." She poured their coffee and set the pot on a brass trivet.

Sharon noticed the long white fingers, devoid of all jewelry. No engagement diamond, no wedding band, ageless hands that seemed so much more competent than her own.

"I can understand why you're pessimistic for yourself," Sharon said quietly.

"But I'm not. You're the one who's giving so much weight to our various circumstances. And who knows," she added, breaking an oatmeal cookie in half. "Maybe you will find Joe Perfect back home in the corn fields."

"It absolutely amazes me that everyone thinks I'm husband hunting." She tapped the rim of her cup impatiently with a teaspoon. "Maybe I've learned my lesson about men? Maybe I'm going home to gather the shreds of my ambition? How does everyone know I'm not a frustrated saxophone player or a public relations tycoon? What is this chintzy apron odor I seem to give off?"

"Well now, Sharon Porter, let's try to be sensible."

Sharon sipped the hot black liquid and let it scald down her throat. "Fine. Be sensible," she said.

"First of all," Leda's tone took on an unexpected quality of gentleness, "the lady editor of Taft Publications is not exactly unknown to us. Through the grapevine, that is."

"I see," Sharon interrupted. "And you think Jay is too strong a dose to get out of the blood so easily."

"Shall we say, a poisoned body tends to be left in a weakened condition and is, therefore, more ready prey to other infections."

Sharon smiled. "You choose lovely, descriptive words."

Behind her, she could sense the first light strokes of dawn beginning to spread upward from the horizon. And here she sat, in the middle of nowhere, making hypothetical talk in a fairy tale house with a blue blue hostess. Her shoes felt pasted to the soles of her naked feet. The dress hung oddly on her sore and bloated muscles. She knew that the lipstick was all chewed off. Her life had become suspended like one of those upside-down rides at Coney Island. And all she could do was grope to find the button that would shift her back into position.

"Anyway, what's the use of being so damned analytical?" Leda said, pouring more coffee into Sharon's cup and half filling her own with milk.

The kitchen door banged open and shut on the middle of Leda's sentence. Ralph stumbled in, bumping against the refrigerator and steadying himself by the handle. "So … the cat runs into the mouse where the cheese is." One end of his shirt hung over his belt. He jabbed at it sloppily. "Hello, mouse." Then, nodding to Sharon, "Hello, cheese."

Sharon could almost hear Leda's jaw set. She saw the shoulders twitch backward.

"Can I get you something?"

Leda's controlled voice told Sharon that her presence was preventing more forceful language. She started to get up. But

Leda's had darted out to touch her knee. She leaned back in the chair again and waited.

"You can get me," Ralph teetered forward, then rocked back to the refrigerator. "...You know what you can get me, sweet procuress."

"Ralph!"

The command in Leda's tone startled Sharon. A thrill of pleasure warmed her, as though she had been given a sneak preview of passions to come.

"Ralph, Ralph, Ralph," his voice singsonged. "I ask you, is it fair for a wife not to share her conquests with her only husband? You, little girl, try to be an impartial witness in this case. Would you say it's too much ..."

"Your wit is bringing the house down." Leda's voice was colder than the coffee Sharon sipped in an effort to appear nonchalant.

"You mean your goddamned whoring'll bring the house down. I'm sick and tired to death of these Friday night forays you make into the flesh market under the guise of the ideal hostess." He shook a white knuckled fist wildly. "There's gonna be an end to it. You'll see."

With a sigh, Leda pushed her chair back and strolled to him. She grabbed his elbows and turned him around, pushing him toward the door.

"Why don't you go on up to bed." She pushed him through the doorway and latched the door when it swung closed.

But Sharon saw that she was breathing hard when she sat down again. Little wrinkles of worry outlined her eyes. The little boy quality had momentarily gone. Sharon saw in its place a tired woman, perhaps thirty-five, who probably wished she were dead.

"Sometimes he gets on my nerves," Leda said with a wry awareness of her understatement.

"What you need," Sharon said, "is a vacation." The statement had begun on an impulse to fill up the silence. Now she listened to the echo of her thought and another took fire behind it. Sharon reached out and pressed Leda's hand. "Why don't you come with me for a week?"

Leda's mouth tilted into a smirk. "To Old Overshoe? Not on your life."

"But, listen, the kids are in school, you said."

"Um hmm."

"So what can Ralph do to you even if he wants to do the worst?"

"Go on."

The flicker of interest encouraged Sharon. "With your money and my reputation back home for Right Thinking, we could build a little fortress that Ralph couldn't dent with any dossier of facts. My uncle is the town minister ..."

"Wait a minute, honey, I'm losing you."

"But it's simple, Leda," she hurried on eagerly. "If you want a divorce, what you need is good reasons and a background to fight him with. I can get you that. All it'll take is a little time, maybe a few months.

Leda crossed her arms and leaned back. "And in return?"

"I need money to get started again," Sharon said, fumbling with her excuse. It sounded tinny even to her own ears. She felt herself about to explode into a fluster of mumblings. She did not really know what it was that she wanted from Leda.

CHAPTER FOUR

They sat in Leda's kitchen talking until sun up.

The sweep of light on a new day seemed to dispel the monsters in Sharon's mind. She thought about going back to her own apartment, of cleaning up and straightening the mess there. Her body ached for sleep, yet she knew it would be best to remain active. Not to lie down, alone, and dream. No, she did not feel up to that yet. Best wait until exhaustion took over. Then she could sleep without dreams.

As though reading her thoughts, Leda said, "Why don't you stay? There's an extra bedroom right next to mine. Complete with shower and towels."

"Thanks, but I don't think so," Sharon said, pushing her cup away. "The sooner I get around to facing it, the better."

"True."

They had gathered the dishes and carried them to the sink before Leda said, "But do me a favor and take the receiver off the hook when you get home."

Sharon's glance darted up to find reassurance on Leda's face.

"No, I'm not joking," Leda said.

"I didn't really think you were," Sharon replied grimly.

Leda began to run water onto a mound of soap suds. "How come you didn't think of it yourself?"

Sharon watched bubbles gather and float lightly around the tops of the dishes. "Frankly, I didn't think Jay considered me worth the effort." She watched Leda scoop suds into a cup. "But now that I think about it, he would give me a hard time.

Yeah, just for the fun of it." She exhaled a breath of air in nervous spurts. "But I'm not afraid of him, Leda. I'd stand right up and kick his face in."

Leda smiled the indulgent smile that smoothed her face into a young boy's. "Would you?" she said.

"I've got to." Sharon snapped up a towel and began to rub a dripping plate.

"Then phone me later on. Will you do that?"

Sharon heard the quiet urgency which, for the first time, betrayed Leda's real interest. So Ralph's accusation was true, after all. A thrill of curiosity tingled deliciously along her lips. No woman had ever felt this way about her before. At least, not as far as she knew. What would it be like, she wondered, to give oneself to this kind of love?

"Yes, I'll call you the minute everything's in order. But it might take me a month." She laughed nervously. "You just don't know the condition things have come to." Impulsively she wanted to ask Leda to come along. But a twinge of embarrassment stopped her. "At the latest, four o'clock," she said softly. "Even if I haven't finished."

Sharon waited till she saw the tiniest spark flash in Leda's eyes. Then, satisfied that she had been understood, she agreed to let Leda drive her home.

Sharon pushed open the door of her apartment and flung herself into the room, her body tensed and ready for the demons that would rise out of the furniture. With fists clenched, she glared around at the wreckage, at the torn shade still flapping out the window, at the drift of dust, tobacco bits and junk.

In a great surge of release, she laughed a great, body shaking series of deep throated tones.

"Goddamn it!" she said and listened for an answer.

But it was true. No one crept out of the walls or the closets. Just a dirty little apartment faced her.

She stepped out of her shoes and kicked them aside. Then she unzipped the dress and let it fall. An old pair of jeans lay tumbled near the floor lamp and she pulled them on, noticing as she buttoned them the two inch difference between the material and her waist. Yes, a long, twisting road it had been since the days of the plump kid from … Old Overshoe. Sharon smiled at the memory of Leda's gentle jibe. That was about the extent of Leda's ability at nastiness. What a pleasure.

The thought of Leda reminded Sharon that she was alone for the time being and she snapped on the radio to music that would keep her spirits high.

For awhile she surveyed the room, wondering where to begin and estimating how long it really would take to clear away three years' worth of degradation. But it had to be done. You couldn't sublet an apartment looking like this.

From the closet beneath the kitchen sink, she brought out the collection of large paper bags that she saved for garbage and began dropping in everything that she met on her travels across the room. Ash trays, pencil stubs, empty cough drop containers. Actually, she thought, it was going to be a cinch. All one had to do was continue not thinking and act like a snow plow.

When the phone rang, Sharon tightened with the thought that it must be Jay. Cursing herself for not having listened to Leda, she took off the receiver and buried it beneath a pillow. Her arms felt stiff with determination. Strength of purpose flowed cool and rapid as the rush of mountain streams she had known. How easy it was to be brave. A matter of bravado. Act the part and along came the feelings to help. She went back to the closet, pulled out the carpet sweeper and banged it against the couch legs in her energy to clean things up.

When the downstairs bell rang, she didn't answer it. Let him ring his head off. Let him split an appendix. If he only knew how immune she felt …

Her palms went slippery on the wooden handle of the sweeper. She clenched her teeth shut. Let him do his worst. There was no law of man or nature that could make her give in to him.

She waited, holding her breath, for the bell to ring again. Minutes she stood, not daring to think that she was safe yet. Then, gingerly, she leaned the sweeper handle against the wall and crept to the window. She would watch to see him going away.

But if she put her head out and he were looking up?

Instead, she stood at the side of the window and took a quick peep. Seeing no one familiar, her courage grew. She leaned out a little further, pressing her knuckles to the gritty sill.

And she was in this position, halfway out on the fire escape, when the door flung open.

She pulled back into the room, grazing her head on the window frame. Yet she hardly felt it. She turned to stare at Jay, solidly planted with feet wide apart, arms folded, his tanned face jagged with shadows from the high bones she had once loved.

A cold thrill of fear jolted along her in tingling tremors. "I told you to stay away from me," she said, her voice high and breathy.

Jay pressed his lips together but he did not move.

She wondered if he had heard her. "Get out." The words were two gasps. "Get out or so help me, I'll kill you."

She felt her head pulsing as though her heart had moved into her skull. Why didn't he answer? Do something? Grab her and beat her? Anything.

"You've got no right to break in on me," she continued, frantic to make him respond.

Sharon leaned back against the window. If necessary, she would climb out on the fire escape and run up to the roof. Make headlines in the paper. Embarrass him. Scandalize him. Wreck his career. Something to get even.

"And what do you think I've come for?" he said finally.

Even across the twenty feet of space that separated them, she could feel the hot, burning coals which were his version of a pleasant manner.

"I don't care. You don't interest me any more. And whatever you've come for, you can't have." Somehow, she still couldn't get her voice louder than a whisper.

He came into the room now, his arms moving to jam hands into the pockets of his corduroys. "Stop acting like a kid."

"I said get out."

Gingerly he stepped around the piles of trash and sat down on the unmade daybed. "Spring cleaning?"

"This is my apartment and you're violating my privacy." Her voice had begun to return. She came away from the window.

"You know something? I don't understand you."

Jay's head tilted sideways and he moved his jaw off-bite in a mannerism familiar to her. It implied that he had ignored everything she'd said.

"You stubborn bastard," she said. "What do I care that you don't understand me? You never have. You never will. And what's more, I don't believe you could, even if you wanted to."

The heat of Sharon's anger dispelled all fear. She felt her heart pumping furiously, sending strength to her limbs, determination to her mind.

"Oh, don't I?" He chuckled a low, satisfied sound. "Seems to me I've understood you pretty well."

The insinuation on his lips made her face go pale.

"Rotten bastard," she muttered.

"You know something," he continued. "I've never heard so many obscenities from you all in one day. I think you're changing, Sharon. I think you're forgetting how to be a lady."

"I'm changing all right," her voice stabbed at him. "And in a lot of ways you wouldn't even dream of."

"For instance."

"I said, none of your goddamned business. Now leave, will you, before there's trouble." She felt a cold tension in her body that seemed to threaten a violence she could not predict.

"Look," he said, "you seem to forget all the time I've put in on you. You don't just walk out of a person's life on a whim like this. No explanations, nothing. What am I, some kind of machine you press the buttons on?"

"That's right. Now take your ego someplace else to be soothed. I told you, I'm not interested."

"Oh, Sharon, Sharon, Sharon."

His voice said her name with a disgust that turned her stomach to mash.

"Go on, go!" she yelled on a shrill, breaking note.

"No, I'm not going anywhere," he said with the stubbornness she had experienced in him so many ways. "Till I understand what you think you're doing and why."

Sharon turned her back on his voice and realized what a mistake it had been not to stay with Leda. She had listened to him and watched him and searched for some indication beneath his surface calm. But she knew that he was tranquil to the core. All she had disturbed was his curiosity. And the most she had inconvenienced was his office routine. He would have to find another editor on short notice. And at best, a good one was hard to come by. She tired to calm her breathing and steady the desolation trembling through her.

"If you came to say I ought to at least stay on the job," she spoke while gazing at the bright sky stretching cloudlessly, "the answer is: nuts to you."

"So you think you've got my number," he said with icy derision. "Try again."

Sharon didn't know what to do with him. "Yes, I think that's it," she said. "You never thought about anything except your comforts and your bank account. Why should you start now? It would be out of character for you, Jay. And believe me, I ought to know by now."

"You know nothing."

The flicker of anger in his voice encouraged her. She felt closer to the sore spot. Maybe soon she would hit it, drive home her own arrows and kill him off for good. "I know nothing?" she repeated. "After chasing you around this fool city for three years, I know plenty."

"Sure, like spreading your legs for any comer."

The words slapped. She whirled around, her lips burning. "I was faithful to you and you know it."

"Oh?"

"That's right. Dope that I was, I trailed after you like a little pup, thinking you'd ask me to marry you one day. That you wanted to make something decent out of the thing that we had. But I watched you, Jay Taft. I watched the bankroll grow and turn you into a … a …" Her voice broke and she pressed her fist to her mouth, biting hard against the bone.

"You saw nothing."

She heard the blind insistence and knew there was no use going on. He didn't want to face the change that had come over him any more than she wanted to face her own degradation.

"All right, Jay," she said more gently. "Let's not argue. There's no point to all this. Why don't you just accept it at face value? I'm not interested any more and that's all there is to say."

The desolation in her voice rang into the silence.

"It's not all that easy," he said, moving to get up. "And frankly, I don't understand how you can be satisfied with such a flimsy excuse."

Sharon saw with growing horror that he was coming toward her. "I don't want you to touch me," she said quickly.

"Why not?" The half smile on his jagged face seemed to challenge her.

"Don't, Jay." She put up her hands in readiness.

"If I don't do things to you any more, what's there to be afraid of?"

He stood right over her now. She could see the movement of his nostrils, their tense pride being held in for a moment.

"Please."

The breath went out of her as he grabbed her by the shoulders and yanked her toward him.

All of her cried out inside. Her stomach seemed to explode in a hot, multi-colored rage of anger and fear and protest. But nothing came out from her lips.

She felt his strong fingers carelessly pull out her shirt and probe along her flesh to tear open the hooks of her brassiere. Her own hands balled into tight fists and she beat out blindly, hitting wherever she found contact. Her body felt light as cotton candy as he lifted her. She bounced once, hard, on the couch. Then he fell on top, pinning her to the musty crumpled sheets. She smelled the stale odor of her own sweat. Nails clawed at her dungarees, dragging them over her hips. She brought up one knee, thinking to catch him in the groin, but his own rock hard thigh straightened her leg and held it. His breath stung her eyelids. Her fists tingled from beating him on shoulders and back without result. *He's raping me,* she thought. And it was a strange nightmare world that teetered into darkness.

Soon, the fury began to ebb from her limbs. Her back ached from the effort of pulling away. Her thighs went flaccid. Little by little, Sharon felt herself slipping. She recognized the hard outline of his hips against her stomach, the insistent, mysterious pressure of his maleness, probing, forcing through to her. With one last twist of her body to escape him, she sighed. All of her seemed to open wide now, accepting, allowing, yielding to the power of his seeking.

Then slowly, slowly, Sharon forgot her promises. The nightmare of him became clouded with the life in her body. Of their own volition, her hips lifted, moving to respond, twisting to help him. Her arms tightened around his back. Perspiration trickled between them. His chin bruised the soft flesh of her breasts.

Beneath them the pillows panted, the old springs groaned. The couch slipped away from the wall as one of her feet hit it. In the midst of her desire, she laughed and kicked at the wall wanting to hurt herself. And then her flesh began to steam. She tightened her legs around his waist.

The sheet beneath them tore in a loud noise.

A slanting afternoon sun played over the droplets of perspiration on her arms, cooling her skin. Slowly she became aware of the traffic sounds outside. She gazed at a pigeon on the rim of the fire escape.

Jay sat on the floor beside her, resting his elbows on his knees. She tried not to look at him, knowing that to face him meant to answer all his questions with an unequivocal *yes*.

Yes ... I love you.

Yes ... I need you.

Yes ... You can make me do anything you want me to do. Anytime you want me.

"Will you be at the office tomorrow?" he said, and she felt he was trying to placate her with this unnecessary formality.

"Yes," she said. "Yes ... yes."

CHAPTER FIVE

She lay alone now, on the bed, straining to hear his footsteps going away from her. The sound of his leather soles fading too fast on the staircase. She visualized him on the second landing, then the first and finally with the sun making a deep squint line between his eyebrows.

So Leda had been right, after all. And there was no way to handle him and win. No way to quench her need, the need he had brought to life in her.

Sharon stretched, wiggling her ankles, trying to think. Her brain felt like a sponge from lack of sleep, her body limp and heavy, sated for the moment, content as a pig.

It was true, she told herself with contempt. The habit of lust was not so easy to break.

But even her self-annoyance felt weak right now. Her eyelids fluttered closed. The world sailed rosily away.

When she finally awoke, the room had begun to fill with shadows. She sat up with a jolt and leaped for the phone, struggling to untangle the cord from beneath the pillow. Her glance darted to the small electric alarm clock lying on its side on a stack of magazines. Six thirty.

Ralph's voice answered the phone and Sharon could tell by its bored weightiness that he was sober.

He was sorry but no, he didn't remember her and Leda was out right now. Could he take a message?

Sharon wondered if he were telling the truth. "When do you expect her?"

He couldn't say. She wasn't one for schedules, you know. Why not try again, say tomorrow morning?

"Yes, I'll do that," she forced her voice to remain as impersonal as his. "But should she call in, my number is …" And Sharon gave it with a low heart. She knew that Ralph wasn't about to aid a relationship that didn't include himself.

Sharon put back the receiver and switched on all the lights, telling herself there was no real difference between daytime and night. That was silly to get nervous now. Kind of late to be nervous, after all. And anyway, what was the worst that could happen to her? She wouldn't be the first woman to ruin her life over a man. And it wasn't much of a life at that.

But resignation wouldn't come. She felt inside herself the struggle for freedom thrashing desperately.

Leda would help her. Leda understood. And Leda cared.

Forcing herself to be steady, Sharon ironed a crumpled shirtwaist dress. No doubt Leda had tried to phone her and found the line busy. Maybe she would try again, knowing that she was home.

After all, Leda was too experienced to think that Sharon had gone back on her word. No doubt, she would know exactly what had happened without being told. The best thing to do would be wash and dress and try to wait. And if she hadn't called by eight o'clock, she would try Kermit and see if he knew where Leda might be.

By eight o'clock the silence whined in Sharon's ears. She stared at the clock and gave it another five minutes.

Then she dialled Kermit, steeling herself for his sarcasm.

But no, he couldn't help her either. Knowing Leda, she might have flown to Montreal for the weekend.

Sharon's last flicker of hope crumbled and died with Kermit's words. It was possible, after all, that Leda had simply shrugged her off when the call hadn't come through. Why should someone with all her money, all her friends and access to the world sit around and wait for one hysterical child still moaning over a man? Leda had her own future to think about.

And so it seemed to Sharon that Jay had managed to ruin everything that she touched.

Yet why was it that no one had ever managed, quite, to ruin Jay? Despite his greed and selfishness, he seemed to have everything that he wanted. Certainly, he didn't miss the home and domestication for which she yearned like such a fool. Why was it that he could be so free about life, so easy-come, easy-go? What did he have that she lacked? Certainly there were plenty of women in New York who played the game of bachelorhood as readily as men. Why couldn't she do it, too? What was to stop her from getting a good job and a harem of men, the way Jay had himself money and a following of women?

For that matter, having met Leda, she could include a few women, too. Liven things up a bit.

A sly smile twisted her lips as she thought what Jay's reaction would be when he found her beating him at his own game.

All she had to do was make a start. And what better time or place to start than right now, out in the warm Spring night?

The jaunty mood carried Sharon outside and as far as Times Square. There were plenty of men who would be glad to oblige her, she knew.

But when she saw their faces, leering in the neon lights of the movie houses, her courage began to waver. She hadn't tried to kid herself that this was what she wanted for a career. But anything was better than sitting home and waiting for the walls to breathe that deadly vapor of loneliness down her neck. When you felt this desperate, you couldn't be too choosy.

She eyed the fat ones and the shabby ones and the sad ones and the sober. Maybe she ought to bolster herself with a drink? No, that would be suicide.

I'll just wait, she thought, *for the first one who asks me.*

But the first one had on the uniform of a foreign navy and didn't speak English very well. She needed to be with people who would be around when she called.

A hell of a thing to try to pick up someone halfway decent on Forty Second Street.

She got into a cab and went back downtown to the Village. Every variety of the human species could be found there, she remembered. Hadn't she lived long enough on the outskirts to know what was what?

The cab circled and Sharon felt her life going round and round again. How low could she bounce before splitting her head open? But she was swirling too fast to catch hold of something strong enough to stop her.

Sharon knew all the Village bars by rote because Jay had dragged her to every one of them.

She fairly tumbled out of the cab when it jerked to a halt. The momentum carried her across the street and inside to face the bartender.

Saturday evening and she stood at an empty counter. Toward the rear, a slim boy shot disks at a pin ball bowling game. The methodical, unthinking action grated on her nerves as the score tallied in hollow clicks. Three minutes later she paid for the untouched beer and walked out.

Another bar. Another bartender's face, white as the towel with which he wiped glasses. Her own face reflected in the blue lighting behind him. She looked drawn and coarse. Her lips seemed a startled red, her eyelids puffy. It seemed to Sharon written all over her face what she had been doing this afternoon.

"Where's everybody?" she said to the bartender.

He shrugged his bald head to one side. "It's early yet."

"Well, when does it pick up?" She sounded too urgent.

He looked at a fingernail and then too casually at her, seeming not to notice the size of her breasts, their roundness beneath the cotton demureness. "Soon," he said. "Wait around."

But she wasn't in the mood for waiting.

A third bar, up two steps...a fourth, through swinging doors...Because she needed people tonight, the city had become a ghost town. Jay's conspiracy with the world to keep her in line. Her throat felt like fingers were pressing against her windpipe.

Perhaps a restaurant.

But she ducked suddenly into a drugstore and phoned Leda again.

And again Ralph answered. A little annoyed this time, his voice cooler, openly aloof. And contemptuous as hell.

Fine one to sneer at her, she thought. Still, he had the edge over her. He was married.

Big deal, being married. Big deal!

She knew her stomach wouldn't hold any food, but it was dinner hour and her chances to make a contact were distinctly better where there was life.

Sharon peered in through half a dozen windows until she found a small Spanish place that seemed crowded because it had so few tables. If the night really became unbearable, she could always come back later for the short, dark waiter trimming his way with an armful of laden dishes. She waited to judge which of the empty tables were part of his station, then, touching her chignon for stray wisps, descended into the subtle aromas of saffron and sea food.

Listlessly, she glanced over the menu, her ears alert for snatches of conversation from other tables. At the right moment, perhaps she could smile or appear to agree with someone. Men were always picking up women. Why couldn't she be the one tonight?

Injecting little phrases of encouragement into her thoughts, Sharon ordered a Martini and paella. She watched the dark-skinned waiter scribbling her order. From the exertion of running back and forth to the kitchen, he was breathing through his mouth. She saw the nick on his front tooth, the slight movements of his Adam's apple above the black bow tie. But he did not seem to notice her in return.

Slowly she ate dinner, picking at the bits of chicken and mussels in the rice. She examined the yellow and green murals splashed around the walls, a dusty guitar hanging precariously above the heads of a young couple huddled in an aura of privacy.

Around her dishes clattered, conversation mingled with giggles. The restaurant was crowded now and yet everyone seemed miles away. Sharon stroked the stem of her Martini glass, then lifted it to her lips, downing the contents in two swallows. The gin burned her throat, but she ordered another.

Blinking to clear her blurred vision, Sharon made her way out of the restaurant and along the pavement that seemed to be jumping farther away from her feet at each step. She stopped to lean against a pyramid of garbage cans. But the street refused to lie down flat and she started to walk again, lifting her feet high above the imaginary folds in the concrete carpet.

I'm off to see the wizard, she mumbled musically, *the wonderful wizard of Oz.* But though she was concentrating hard on getting to the corner, Sharon had no idea where she was going to go from there.

Nor did it bother her. A happy feeling of security cuddled her. She felt sure that just around the next corner someone waited for her. Someone tall and strong and friendly. Her thighs began to tighten.

The alcohol sloshed in her stomach and tickled along the insides of her legs. She felt her breasts begin to ache inside the cups of her brassiere.

I'm off... to see... the wizard... The sound of her voice swirled inside her head. She stretched out one palm and pressed it against the rough bricks of an old building. Her body yearned to lie down on a pile of feathers, naked in a Mediterranean sunshine.

As she continued to sing, pictures began to form in her imagination. Pictures of herself in the arms of eager men who did not know her name. She could see herself vividly, feel them against her, wanting her, probing her gently, then harder, to please her. Her hand against the brick became a fist and she hit at it, trying to force the pictures away, trying to stifle the wracking need that surged furiously now beyond control.

She did not know who he was or how he had found her.

She did not recognize the tan wall paper, the vague smell of onions, the lumpy mattress pressing between her shoulderblades.

But his thick arms felt hard and smooth and slippery with the sweat of her palms. His wide chest curved slightly above her and she pressed her nose along its center ridge. He seemed to spread above her endlessly. The voice of a news commentator vibrated two glasses in rhythm with his speech.

"Turn that damn thing off," she muttered.

"It's next door," he said. "Forget it."

She felt her thoughts shatter away with the pressure of his lips against her own. Something bristled and she knew he had a mustache.

And she knew he needed her. His hands felt along her body like a miser's sifting greedily in gold. He explored rapidly, in quick movements as though there were not time enough to know it all. She heard his soft whispering of obscenities as he touched her. He seemed to transform her body into a delicious forbidden fruit. She began saying the words along with him. Her hands followed his, fondling her own flesh, coming for the first time to know it through his male appreciation.

He seemed to stretch out the need in her, longer, interminably. Her own desire wound snakelike, squeezing her body and relaxing it.

"Do something," she gasped finally.

Her own hands reached to guide him.

With wild force, she plunged him deep. A little scream escaped her lips. Her back curved bowlike, pushing him upward with the new strength of her craving.

Every muscle in her quivered tautly. She tore at his skin trying to urge him into a faster tempo. Words tumbled incoherently, dribbling out the side of her mouth.

And when he slowed, she would not let him go.

"Stay with me," she whispered on a breath of pleading, her ankles locked around him.

A misty dawn touched her scalp with damp weight. Slowly it turned to a damp drizzle.

"Come on, toots, I've got to get to work."

Sharon felt him pulling away from her. She released her hold and began to dress.

They walked together into the street and she saw him dash through traffic to catch a bus.

The drizzle became harder. She felt the rain soaking through to her scalp. She walked along, her glance flicking over the piles of Sunday papers protected by a canopy. What kind of work did a man do on Sunday? The question floated like an aimless balloon, occupying her for some minutes.

Then it faded as she remembered the night. An overwhelming desire to scrub her skin with a wire floor brush wracked through her guts.

CHAPTER SIX

The round clock in a barber shop window said eight thirty. Another long day stretched ahead, meaningless and dull as the rain. A steady pounding of desolation thudded along with the heavy drops falling on the slanted canopy above. She stood for awhile observing the dash of persons from doorway to doorway. A faint odor of Spring earth wafted on an early morning gust. The freshness seemed to blow through her, aerating, cleansing away some of the memories.

She went into the candy store and ordered an ice cream soda, needing the feel and taste of cold, bubbly liquid. She swung around on the stool, debating whether or not to try to call Leda at this hour. Supposing she got Ralph again? The memory of his thinly disguised hostility still prickled. And if she made a nuisance of herself, Leda would get the brunt of his anger. Better to wait awhile.

From the rack of paper backs, she lifted out a volume and skimmed the chapters. How strange it felt to fan down the paragraphs without an editorial pencil. Strange and pleasant. She would have to get a job far away from the publishing world. Too brutal, too uncertain. Too reminiscent of Jay.

A round old lady in two sweaters and dirty apron wrapped twice around her middle took the change. "Fine weather for ducks," she said, dropping the coins into one jingling, bulging pocket.

Sharon gazed past the dripping, scalloped canopy to the streaming asphalt. The thin cotton of her dress felt plastered to her back. She knew there would be no taxis cruising on this semi-deserted street.

"Can you give me some dimes?" she said and put a dollar bill on the counter.

"I don't know what I got," the woman replied above the no-sale ring of the register.

Sharon took the handful of change and picked around the bundles of magazines and newspapers to a phone booth almost hidden behind tall, empty cartons. She dialed Leda's number and listened to it ring. Absently, her fingers piled and rearranged the coins on the shelf. She felt crouched, ready to spring if Ralph should try to interfere.

But the voice that answered was Leda's, heavy, sluggish with sleep.

"Thank God it's you," Sharon breathed.

"Who is this?" the voice demanded.

Sharon paused before the wedge of its annoyance. "You couldn't have forgotten. Not so soon. Sharon Porter, don't you remember? We sat in your kitchen until ..."

"Yes, yes." The pause of a long yawn. "But this is Sunday." She made it sound as though years had elapsed.

"Didn't Ralph tell you?" Sharon persisted. "I've been trying to reach you all weekend. He said you were away. That he didn't know when you would be back or where to reach you."

"I've been here all weekend." The flat statement of fact seemed to accuse Sharon.

"But it's true. He answered the phone every time. Don't you believe me?"

There was a pause. She could almost hear Leda sliding back under the covers to her more interesting dreams.

"You've got to believe me. I need to see you, Leda. Look, it was my fault that I overslept on Friday and didn't get to work ..."

"Overslept? Friday?"

"Oh, never mind," Sharon said impatiently. "I'll tell you about it when I see you."

"Save it for next week's *Times*," Leda said.

"Don't hang up on me. Please." Sharon's voice seemed to hook onto something and she could not get it loose to continue.

"Well?" Leda said.

Sharon swallowed, trying to steady herself. "Won't you see me today?"

"You make it sound like a catastrophe. All right."

"Make it as soon as you can?"

"Yes."

Sharon felt the glow of Leda's agreement spreading through to warm her. "I'll wait for you right where I am." And she gave the address of the store.

She stepped out of the booth and bought a couple of magazines. It would take Leda at least forty five minutes to dress and drive down. Three-quarters of an hour to hang suspended in the middle of nowhere. She sauntered to the door and pretended to study the sky.

"Not gonna stop so soon," the woman said. She pushed an old rag along the counter, wiping away invisible crumbs. "You ain't got no umbrella neither."

"I just called a friend to come and get me," Sharon said, hoping to soften her.

"Good idea."

As the yellow hands of the Coca Cola ad clock moved toward nine, the narrow store began to crowd. Men with walking shorts visible through their transparent raincoats, girls in oversized army pants, purchasers of cigarettes and newspapers, other dawdlers like herself. The minutes dragged as the store became livelier. Community Sunday. She could almost smell the odor of breakfast toast from these comfortable people, sense the routine of their days, the families they took for granted, the goals toward which they moved. And she?

The gray Jaguar appeared beyond the rain smeared door. Sharon pushed through and rushed out, running through puddles to cross the street. Her fingers fumbled with the cold, wet handle. She saw Leda lean across and pull it open from the inside.

She flung herself onto the deep red leather and leaned back, panting, strands of hair plastered across one cheek, blinking through droplets of water on her lashes.

"I thought you'd never get here," she gasped.

Leda started the motor again and pulled carefully into the growing stream of automobiles. "Pull yourself together, child."

Her voice sounded cold as the rain, but Sharon knew it was only surface. "I wish I knew what it took to grow up," she said.

"That's an easy one," Leda smiled. "Time."

"Very funny."

"Anyway," Leda glanced up to her rear view mirror, "where shall we take you? Home?"

"Not mine," Sharon said.

"No, I didn't mean yours." She wore a gray cable stitch slipover and navy slacks, revealing lithe outlines that hardly made her seem the mother of two children.

"You look so comfortable," Sharon breathed.

"That's an easy one, too," Leda said. "What size are you, about ten?"

Sharon smiled. "The practised eye. But frankly, Leda, I'd rather not run into Ralph this morning. My morale couldn't cope with it."

"Oh, don't worry. He's gone upstate to see the kids."

"Without you?"

"Yeah," her voice sounded tired. "He says it's best for each of us to see them alone. So that they don't have to make a choice. Funny, isn't it, forcing infants to take sides?" She pushed the directional signals and turned a corner. "If I ever hated him for anything, it's for that."

Leda's words quieted Sharon. For the moment, her own problems seemed to fade. She took a handkerchief from her purse and dabbed at the water dripping down her forehead.

The low-throated hum of the motor filled in the pause of their conversation. Sharon watched the slog of the wipers curving in unison across the windshield. A pack of cigarettes on the seat slid toward her as Leda turned the car onto Madison Avenue. How comfortable to sit here, protected from the weather, moving casually toward warmth and bodily comforts. Today, at least, stood some chance of being pleasant.

"I never did get the apartment cleaned," Sharon said, wanting to rebuild the bridge of their friendship.

"Oh?"

She heard the merely formal interest and felt a twinge of embarrassment. How foolish, how egocentric to have believed that anyone could take her petty problems seriously.

"I suppose there's a woman leaving some man every minute," she said with an effort at humor. "You know, like a baby being born?"

"No doubt," Leda responded in warm agreement.

The cool, slender fingers on the wheel seemed capable of overcoming such matters. Certainly, a love affair couldn't have the same capacity to hurt as the loss of one's children. But what could she do to help Leda solve her problems, when her own were so far beyond her?

"Well, what do you know," Leda said cheerfully as they reached the house. "There's my parking space."

They ran the few steps to the door and Leda pushed it open without a key.

The rooms sprawled before them, silent and empty. All traces of party had been cleaned away. By contrast this morning, the livingroom's vast size with groupings of wing chairs, heavy oak table and crystal chandelier gave a feeling of sedateness to the household.

"It's not the same place without people," Sharon said with a touch of amusement.

Leda dropped herself into a red leather chair and put her feet up on a hassock. "Is anywhere?"

Sharon shrugged. For all the space, she could find no comfortable corner for herself.

"I thought all small town people knew the art of relaxing," Leda said, observing her. "Now take me for instance, brought up in the center of this hell hole. I can catnap anywhere, any time." She grinned and the aloof tone melted in the warm depths of her eyes. "But you. You look like you haven't slept for days."

"Why should I?" Sharon smiled back. "I haven't." She saw Leda's eyebrow arch questioningly. "Maybe I'm even more nervous than you think." The flippant tone seemed to fall flat beneath Leda's scrutiny. Finding no words to continue, she searched in the bottom of her purse for cigarettes but found only a crumpled, empty package. "It's been an active weekend," she said, dropping cellophane into an ash tray.

Leda pushed a silver box toward her. "I can imagine," she said. "Maybe you want to talk about it?"

"No," Sharon sighed. "I'd rather not relive it. All I want is a plane ticket out of here."

"Now, now," Leda clucked.

"I guess I deserve to have you make fun of me. But I can't seem to come up with anything clever or useful or just plain sensible." As she talked, her body began to remind her of its aching muscles, its flayed nerves. Her voice became shaky, her throat tightened. The patter of rain against the windows seemed to isolate her from the world, its love, its aspirations.

Leda stroked ash from her own cigarette. "Why don't we start with something practical like a nice, hot bath? That ought to relax you a little."

Sharon felt her face flush. "I didn't come here to ..."

"...take advantage of the facilities?" Leda waved her wrist limply. "But why not? They come with the apartment."

While Sharon objected, Leda took her upstairs into a high ceilinged room of small gray tiles. The huge bath tub stood on claw and ball feet. On the opposite wall, a row of light blue towels hung above the grating of a fireplace.

"Enjoy yourself," Leda said. "I'll bring you some slacks and a shirt." Before Sharon could answer, she pulled the door closed.

Why not?

Sharon unbuttoned her dress and turned the faucets on full. From a wall tray above the rim, she took a blue sponge and floated it on the water. A tiny bottle of bath oil lay in the tray. She unscrewed its cap and sniffed. The faint, fresh odor pleased her and she shook a few drops into the tub. Then she closed her eyes and stretched her legs, feeling the water stroke the bruises on her thighs.

A peacefulness engulfed her as she imagined Leda going through her closet for something that would fit. How lovely to know that there was someone near who was trying to help.

She lathered the sponge and rubbed her skin with energy, trying to scrape off its surface of cells. Sharon watched the skin growing red and rubbed harder, dissolving the memory, dissolving last night, dissolving the strange drive inside her that was destroying her good sense.

Then she turned herself in the tub, opened the drain plug and slid her shoulder under the tap, watching the crystal water course down her shoulder and over one breast, leaping off the point of her nipple.

Sharon was huddled in this position when Leda came in, a red and white garment hanging over her arm.

The two women looked at each other, neither of them speaking for a moment. Sharon felt the force in Leda that kept the woman's eyes fixedly on her own. A flush of heat came to her cheeks, distinctly separate from the water's steam.

"I thought you might want to take a nap first," Leda said evenly. She hung the pajamas on a hook and a pale blue bathrobe of silk over them.

"Blue's your favorite color, isn't it?" Sharon said to fill the awkward pause.

Leda nodded. "Baby blue. I had a friend once who used to wear it all the time."

"Before you got married," Sharon said, not needing an answer.

"Yes," Leda echoed, "before."

A twist of anger spun through Sharon. It went through her like a comet, nor could she account for its presence. She sat up and turned off the faucets and stood in the tub. "Will you throw me a towel, please?" she said in a manner meant to be nonchalant.

The towel came sailing at her from where Leda stood beside the fireplace.

She wrapped it around her body and began to rub vigorously till her skin tingled. Smudges of black and blue marks dotted her body and she made no attempt to hide them. While she dried herself, she stared coldly across at Leda, daring her to express some tinge of interest.

"So, you really have had a busy weekend," Leda said, a tilt of mockery on her lips.

"All work and no play makes Jack a dull girl," Sharon said with all the acid she could muster. "And I'll tell you this," Sharon continued, hoping to keep her lead in this mysterious game. "I wouldn't care if I never slept with another man for as long as I lived."

She saw Leda's head tilt to follow the movement of her foot. "I'll bet."

"No, I mean it."

"Why?"

"Because they're all bastards." Sharon lifted one breast and patted the skin dry beneath it. "There's no fun having sex with selfish, gluttonous bastards who think all women are dirt."

Leda scraped a match on the grating and brought the flame up to a cigarette. "Sounds like a self-appraisal to me," she said softly.

"Why don't you believe it?" Sharon said shakily.

Leda came over and took the towel from her, handing over a can of lilac powder and the pajamas. "Instinct, my dear. Just plain, old instinct."

Sharon started to protest. But she had already ceased to care who won the little game going on between them. The silk material felt cuddly, whispering against her skin in light folds. Barefoot, she walked across the warm tile and tied the bathrobe on, pulling the cord tight around her waist.

She knew without asking that Leda would stay with her while she slept.

CHAPTER SEVEN

Luxuriously, Sharon sprawled across Leda's double bed. The foam rubber mattress held and supported her weight, drawing the fatigue from her limbs. Pulling the blanket to her chin, she stroked her cheek against the soft cashmere. A steady patter of rain tapped peacefully, lulling her thoughts.

Through heavy eyelids, she watched Leda sitting at the far window. Gray light suffused the edges of the woman's profile. She seemed part of the dream into which Sharon was floating.

"Leda?"

"Hmm?"

"What are you doing?"

"Watching the rain."

Sharon moved a foot and sighed. The taut, fresh linen stroked her calves where the pajamas had rolled up. Acres of bed seemed to stretch around her.

"Leda?"

Sharon saw the head turn and an elbow move off the windowsill. She felt Leda's gaze traversing the distance between them.

"Does my sitting here bother you?"

"No, of course not," Sharon's words mumbled into the blanket. She felt the warm vapor of her own breath and knew she ought to move her head higher onto the pillow. She stirred, but the drowsy sensation of sinking pulled at her. "Leda."

The name sounded loud to her own ears but she knew it was hardly a whisper. She wanted the woman near her, beside her on the bed. Close. Close, where she could feel her presence while she slept.

The sound of muted footsteps approached. Sharon smiled upward at Leda's round and serious eyes, made darker by the crease of interest between her brows.

"What's the matter, baby?" Leda murmured, leaning over.

Sharon's fingertips wiggled out from the side of the blanket and touched Leda's knee. Mutely she watched the tightness in Leda's mouth begin to relax.

"So that's it," Leda murmured.

She sat down on the edge of the bed. Encouraged, Sharon let her hand slide across to touch the woolen slacks against Leda's thigh.

"Stay with me," Sharon said, her eyes closed now, her mood easier, nearer to sleep as she felt the rhythm of Leda's breathing.

Cool fingers worked inside the collar of her pajamas and started to massage her neck. "Sleep now."

Leda's words seemed to come from far away, yet she felt secure in the woman's presence. Sharon draped one arm over Leda's leg as though to hold her there while she slept. Bit by bit, she could feel her body giving itself to rest. Her focus on Leda blurred away, floating off to mingle with the snap and brush of wet leaves against the window...

Sharon awoke to a tingling along her arm. Instinctively she drew it from beneath the weight of her own body, slapping and squeezing the muscles. Then she lay back again in the darkness, slowly piecing together the events which had brought her to this room.

But she felt too comfortable for thinking. The knots had worked out of her body and in their place she felt a warm resilience. A smile of relief and pleasure stirred through her thoughts as she became aware of Leda's breathing from the other side of the mattress. Leda, too, had fallen asleep. Probably needed it.

For a long while she lay quite still, not wanting to waken the woman who had been so good to her.

Sharon brought her arms out into the cool air and listened to the roll and squeal of tires on wet asphalt moving slowly along Lexington Avenue. The Sunday night congestion of homebound traffic. Home. Family. Routine. A second's uneasiness tweeked through her. She nuzzled over closer to Leda, who insisted on sleeping so heavily.

Sharon wished Leda would wake up. The day had disappeared down a hallway of dreams, but nothing was settled. Soon it would be tomorrow and tomorrow meant Jay once more. Jay looking for her, finding her. Using her for his pleasure.

But she had promised herself to stop it somehow, even if it took ten years to find strength enough to fight him.

If only there were someone to take his place. Someone to quiet the outrage of desire that assailed her even now, that seemed to be ever lurking, ever demanding release. If only…

Through the shadows, Sharon stared at the back of Leda's head, its fluff of short curls dishevelled like a child's. She had fallen asleep in her clothes. The sweater was pulled up along her back, revealing an area of skin just visible in the darkness. Tantalizing to touch, to know, to see with one's fingertips.

Sharon's body moved closer. The blanket still separated them, restraining her from a sudden, wild desire to throw herself into Leda's arms, to give herself to Leda's kind of love. To lose herself, become one with the peace and the maturity. One with the experience and the calm to take life as it happened.

Very lightly, Sharon touched the woman's shoulder. Her fingertips moved along the design of the cable stitching. She hardly realized where her hand explored. When it moved over the swell of one breast, she pulled it quickly away. And shuddered with a strange deliciousness.

The darkness gave Sharon courage. Her thoughts danced like luminous elves.

Her hand began to creep again along Leda's back. She felt the bony curve of her spine, the warm smoothness of skin. The outline of ribs that moved in gentle rhythm as she slept.

Sharon pulled herself closer and laid her cheek to the woman's shoulder. A subtle perfume of lilac came from Leda's clothes. It seemed to beckon, to urge Sharon on.

She found the elastic band of Leda's brassiere and paused. If she opened the hooks, certainly Leda would feel it and waken. Would she turn and smile and draw Sharon close?

Sharon held her breath. She felt the bra give way. One firm breast slid clear of its release. Her palm cupped to meet it.

Sharon quivered with sudden fear. She had never touched a woman. Not like this. And yet, as she felt the weight of the flesh against her hand, it seemed so natural. So right to be lying here, close to love, close to warmth, close to gentleness.

And still, irritatingly, Leda continued to sleep.

Sharon molded herself around the relaxed body, bending her knees upward, holding Leda as though the woman were sitting in her lap. She lay her head behind Leda's on the pillow. Ever so lightly, she grazed her lips along the soft hairs at the nape of Leda's neck. Her hand tensed with the need to probe further, to seek out and find the knowledge of Leda's body.

Hesitating, slow, she searched down along the flat belly. Her hand met and stopped at the belt of Leda's slacks. Carefully, she played with the buckle, pulling it gently open. Curiosity tingled and churned on itself, goading Sharon. She half wished that Leda would come awake and slap her. But even when Leda turned in sleep, Sharon paused only for the moment.

At last she had the slacks unzipped. Her palm roamed over the silky underwear, along the band of elastic, across the curve of stomach, and lower.

Sharon held her breath.

Again Leda turned, flinging one arm wide. Her thighs lay spread now, her body accessible.

Sharon tried to see through the darkness, wanting somehow to impress the knowledge of her desire on Leda's brain. She put her lips to the woman's ear and whispered her name. She touched the tip of a warm earlobe with her tongue, then held it between her lips.

With sudden, violent need, she shook her, then fell back as Leda came wide awake and sat up.

"What is it?" she said with an urgency that sent Sharon into anxious silence.

After a pause, Leda shook her head and exhaled a long note of relief. "I dream," she said lightly, "stories you wouldn't be able to edit with a straight face."

"What do you mean?" Sharon said breathily. She wanted to keep Leda talking long enough to hide her own confusion, to hide the tremble of frustration that would give away her desires.

"I'd better not tell you," Leda said, "or you'd call me an old designing lecher."

Sharon remained silent. A flush of warmth came to her cheeks and forehead so that she felt thankful for the darkness. She remembered how it felt, to come awake beneath Jay's touch, to discover that one's dreams were not dreams at all.

But then again, why hide it? Why all this coyness? Neither of them were children.

Once again, Sharon reached out a hand until it touched Leda's arm. Slowly she moved the sweater up to Leda's elbow. "You weren't dreaming," she said in a shaky voice.

Sharon heard a quick intake of breath and waited. But Leda sat perfectly still.

"I'm not exactly your type," Leda said.

"That's blunt enough." Sharon felt her throat choking up with the bitter taste of pride.

"What I mean is," Leda continued, moving now a little closer, "I'm no good for rebounds. You wouldn't want to bounce off Jay, off Kermit and off me all in one fast weekend, would you? What would it do to our friendship?"

The mockery seemed to float like incense between them.

"I'd better be getting dressed," Sharon said stiffly, barely getting the words out.

She tried to fling herself from the bed.

"Wait a minute," Leda's hand grabbed her wrist. "I said, wait."

Sharon sat with her back to the woman.

"I know how you feel and believe me, I didn't mean for it to come out that way. But you've got to understand me, Sharon. Whatever else I am ..."

"You don't have to explain," Sharon blurted.

"But, baby, I want to."

They seemed to Sharon like ghosts sparring in the darkness. Perhaps the rain would blow in and dissolve the pain so immediate, so real in contrast with their shadows.

Sharon struggled to hold herself in place while Leda tugged at her arm. "Please ... let's not make a thing of this." She wanted to keep her manner flippant, but she heard the break in her voice.

Then she heard Leda moving across the bed toward her.

"Will you listen?" Leda said.

"I don't need you to tell me how wrong this is."

"Wrong? My God, it's got nothing to do with school girl morals."

Sharon felt a cigarette being put into her palm and she lifted it to her lips. A match flared. She saw the brief flash of Leda's profile. A tingle chased through Sharon's skin. So unreal, so beautiful, the voice in the darkness. She felt she could draw Leda's soul into her own body the way she drew in the cigarette smoke.

"To be perfectly frank," Leda continued, "I don't want you to have the pleasure of my husband's interruption."

The truth lay flat and ugly before them.

"Always a man," Sharon breathed. "Somehow or other, there's always a man around to louse up my plans."

"Speak of the devil," Leda said, her fingers tightening around Sharon's.

They sat without speaking, alerted to the sound of a car pulling up in front of the house.

"I'd better get dressed," Sharon said.

Anger propelled her from the bed.

"The light switch is near the door," Leda said.

Sharon stumbled around the furniture, banging her toes but feeling nothing of the pain. Her head seethed with curses, her chest constricted in frustration. The memory of Ralph's voice cut through her, laying open a raw wound.

Her fingers groped along the molding and flicked on blossoms of light around the room as three lamps came to life. "Well?" Her glance darted to Leda. "You're not just going to lie there." An edge of harshness tightened her lips.

"Why not?"

"Why not?" Sharon sucked in her breath.

"Exactly." Leda folded her arms and crossed her legs at the ankles.

"For heaven's sake, Leda." The words tumbling through Sharon's head would not speak out.

"Your dress is in the laundry downstairs, where I hung it to dry. Ralph is on his way up this very minute. There's nothing we can do."

The calmness in Leda's manner slapped at Sharon icily. "But we haven't done anything for him to …" Her voice trailed away in hopelessness as she watched Leda shrug.

There was nothing more to say. Both of them knew Ralph. His unreasoned jealousy still echoed in Sharon's head. Her skin went cold in long fingers of apprehension.

"But I can't stand here like this. Naked."

A wry smile touched Leda's eyes. "Circumstantial evidence?" she said. "But you're way ahead of yourself, baby. Those pajamas cover you quite completely."

Sharon felt a quick flush of embarrassment. The pajamas did cover her body. But the guilt of her thoughts stood out bare. "You know what I mean," she stuttered. "Have you a robe...or something?"

"In the closet behind you."

Sharon whirled and pulled back the sliding door.

"All the way to the right," Leda directed.

Sharon swung out the camel colored robe and flung it on, pulling the cord tight.

But even the robe could not protect her from the trap in which she had caught herself. On one side lay Leda. Helpful, mocking, tantalizing. Innocent until proven guilty. On the other side, coming up the stairs, Ralph. As much as she hated him, she could not deny his right to protect the fragments of his home life in any way possible.

"I don't want to get you into trouble," Sharon said, realizing the foolishness of her words, their futility.

Leda seemed not to hear her. She ran one hand nervously through her hair. An apparent last minute effort to seem decent, Sharon thought. Unconsciously, they both turned toward the door and waited.

It seemed like years before the knock came. The gentlemanly touch of knuckles against wood.

"Leda?"

Sharon had never heard his voice filled, as it was now, with tender questioning. In one word, she could feel the misery, the twisted love, the life Ralph had wanted. Her hand crept up to the lapels of the bathrobe and clutched them.

"What is it?" Leda called, and in contrast, her voice was harsh.

"Can I come in?"

Sharon's glance darted across to the woman. Outlined against the oyster colored walls, she seemed taller, thinner, dissected down to the nerves.

Leda strode across the room, her step on the rug firm.

She's done this before, Sharon thought. But it was a brief sensation that changed into fear as she heard Leda say:

"Can't it wait until later? I've someone with me."

Silence.

And in the silence, Sharon could almost see Ralph's jaw growling hard, the puffy redness bloating out his cheeks.

"You can come out a minute," he said, the words wooden. "I've got a message for you. From Tony."

The firmness in Leda's stance seemed to crumble though she did not move. "In the morning," she said hoarsely.

"From Tony," he repeated. "Your youngest son, Leda. Remember him?"

Sharon could feel the knife twisting inside Leda. One hand reached out and clung to the doorknob.

"All right, Ralph. Give me a second."

The blood had drained from beneath Leda's tan. She put her fingertips to her eyelids and held them there for a second. Then, consciously, she straightened her shoulders.

From the other side of the door, she could hear the fading blur of their voices. Obviously, Leda had walked him down the hall. To spare her the knowledge of their conversation? To hide something from her? To share the remnants of their parental privacy? Sharon could not tell which.

An emptiness haunted her. She sauntered back to the open closet and surveyed absently the row of dresses, slacks and jackets hanging from their mahogany shoulders. How idiotic the world was. How helpless. She had come here to cling to Leda. But Leda herself needed someone for moral support. Was there no place in the world safe and simple?

Sharon unhooked a pair of dark green slacks and stepped into them. A little tight across the hips. But decent enough for this household. Then she opened bureau drawers till she found a white turtle neck sweater. No use hiding in this room all night. No use trembling because of a lost sheep like Ralph. What, after all, could Ralph really do to her?

Nothing that hadn't been done to her already.

Sharon felt the beginning of optimism stretch beneath the weight of her troubles. She had bounced so low that any lower would bring only fame and fortune from Ripley's Believe It or Not.

Sharon opened the door and started down the hall, following the direction of their voices.

The sudden change in her mood seemed to be living a life of its own and dragging her along. What would she do when faced with Ralph? What would she say in the blast of his accusations?

No answer came to mind. Only a conviction that everything was going to work out when the moment came. A giddy confidence twinkled in her expectations. Barefoot, she crossed the hall, following the trail of their voices to the music room.

For a moment, she stood listening to the low argument looming between them. Sharon could feel the restraint, the struggle tearing at each. To step into the middle would be an act of bravado. Yet the bubbling stream of confidence inside her urged her on.

Without knocking, she opened the door.

Words stopped abruptly and both heads snapped around to look at her.

"Hello, Ralph," Sharon said in a sunny voice. "I don't guess you're surprised."

He was standing at the record player and for a moment, Sharon thought that he would spring the distance to her neck. Yet she smiled, took a cigarette from the low table and motioned for Leda's lit one.

Leda pushed herself back against the sofa, wanting apparently to sink into the cushions and disappear.

"Come on, honey, give me a light," Sharon said, ignoring the smudges of misery that had deepened beneath Leda's eyes. "You'll pardon me for interrupting," Sharon flung the words like baubles, "but I don't see that there's anything to hide." She twirled in front of Ralph, conscious of his glare as he took in Leda's clothes on her more rounded body. "Really there isn't." She puffed out a cloud of smoke. "As Leda said ... circumstantial evidence."

"Just what are you trying to do?" Leda's words stuttered brokenly.

"Clear you, of course," Sharon said, still looking directly at Ralph. "Since there's nothing to hide," she lifted her chin, "why should I stay in the bedroom? That makes everything look so guilty."

Sharon had never seen Ralph sober before. And sober, his face had a sharpness very unlike the bloated child Sharon had expected. In the single light that came up from behind the couch, she could see his large, sparkling eyes. "You remind me a little of Jay with that look," she said and tried to laugh above the words. "Just a very little."

She could sense his shallow breathing beneath the herringbone overcoat he still wore. His lips hung slightly open as though frozen on a curse. Instinctively, she knew that all human thought had flown from him. That, like a protective wolf, he stood between her and his family.

Her palms began to perspire. "I tell you that nothing happened," she blurted. "Nothing at all. I needed company, Ralph, and your wife spent the day with me, but ..."

"Nothing at all," Ralph said in a monotone.

Speechless, Sharon watched the snakelike glitter in his eyes. "Well, what are you going to do?" she laughed above her fear. "Kill us? If you don't want to believe it, that's your business. And frankly, I wouldn't make any kind of fuss for your sake, believe me. Or even my own." She drew again deeply on the cigarette. "But I don't see why Leda has to be an innocent victim of your insane jealousy, you fool. Nothing happened and that's the God's honest truth. Take it or leave it. I'd better go," she said to Leda softly. "And I'm sorry I managed to cause all this..." Sharon waved one arm helplessly.

Yet even as she spoke, Sharon's gaze caught it. In the same instant, she knew that Ralph's gaze had caught it, too. She felt him leap across the room behind her, his thick body lunging for the couch.

There was nothing to say as he pulled out her girdle from beneath the cushion.

The three watched in silence as it dangled from Ralph's finger. Sharon felt the vibrations of his triumph as he drew a long, tremulous breath through tightening lips.

"I'm going to get you, Leda," he said, ignoring Sharon. "You know that I'm going to get you once and for all."

"I tell you it means nothing," Sharon screamed. "That's from the other night. With Kermit. You know I was here with Kermit." She leaped at him and grabbed his coat sleeve. "You even saw us go up the stairs."

But she felt Ralph staring through her as though she had not spoken. His fury burned through to Leda, intent, determined, sure of revenge.

Sharon stepped away from him. "But it's not true," her voice fell to a whisper. "Not true at all."

"Forget it, baby," Leda said. "He can't believe anybody any more."

Sharon sat down heavily beside Leda on the couch. Irrevocably, they had mingled their lives together. And Sharon knew there was no escape for herself alone.

CHAPTER EIGHT

"What's he going to do to us?"

Leda's sandals slapped against Sharon's bare heels as they walked through a heavy mist that had settled out of the rain. The wide avenue lay deserted in the pre-dawn cold. An occasional taxi whined past, reminding Sharon that this really was New York and not a nightmare.

"I don't know," Leda said simply. "I never could anticipate the way his mind works. Start legal proceedings, maybe. Or just save it up until he really loses his temper someday."

The hollowness told Sharon that Leda did not much care at this moment. She felt glad for her own presence of mind to get out of the house before Ralph let loose any further.

"But he loves you," Sharon said. "That's kind of a protection against anything rash."

"Yeah?" Leda's shoulders hunched and she dipped one hand into the pocket of her raincoat. "Try reading the newspapers."

Sharon had spoken on a whim and now she clamped her mouth shut. An overwhelming desire to cradle Leda close warmed through her. "You've been so good to me," she said, almost to herself. "You'll never know how really sorry I am."

"It wasn't your fault. Just the wrong timing, that's all." Droplets of mist glimmered on the crest of her curls. "It could have been anyone."

"Thanks," Sharon said. But she did not feel released. She turned up the collar of the polo coat and put her cheek to it, thoughtfully. "Anyway, you can't go back there tonight, that's for sure."

Sharon spoke with a conviction as though she herself were Leda. The touch and odor of Leda's body engulfed her through Leda's clothes, lending her Leda's personality, Leda's sadness, Leda's need for an answer.

"Perhaps not."

Sharon felt the impact of Leda's understatement and knew suddenly the impending violence, the past violence in the woman's life.

"You'll come back with me," she said, "to my place."

"And help you clean up?"

Sharon nodded and they exchanged a smile. Flip flop world. Up today, down tomorrow. But she remembered still the feel of Leda's flesh, the outline's of Leda's breast against her palm, the sleeping calmness awaking into passion. The memory, out of time, out of place, burst into flower.

Sharon pressed her hands in their pockets to her hips to hold herself steady. "Let's take a cab," she muttered and peered through the mist for the movement of a yellow light.

The pungent odor of garbage twitched at Sharon's nostrils as they climbed the stairs to her apartment. She had forgotten what it smelled like here. Forgotten almost the creaking, greasy bannister, the dim bulbs hanging naked above alternate landings.

When she opened her door, the tumble of her apartment seemed to leap out at her. She pulled on the hall light and surveyed the strange, yet familiar jumble of possessions.

"Well, here it is," she said. "Three years worth of nothing."

"Let's try closing that window," Leda said and picked her way across to where the shade still flapped like the wing of a lame bird.

"Can you stand it?" Sharon hesitated to say all the excuses leaping to her lips.

The window came down with a squeak. "I'll try," Leda smiled.

"I don't know how you rich people get to be so versatile," Sharon continued nervously. "If I were brought up in your surroundings, I'd go running out of here holding my nose." She wanted to make it sound funny. Anything to cover the sensation sliding up and down her legs, catching at her stomach, dragging at her arms.

"The middle classes are so damned narrow minded," Leda said, dropping her coat over the table radio. "I don't know how we rich people can bear you."

The familiar mockery reassured Sharon. It seemed to bolster the desolation facing Leda. With mockery she could conquer anything, anyone. Mockery cut the legs off giants. It seemed to stroke Sharon with hope. "Maybe that's why I never had my family come down here," she said, glad for any conversation. "They'd be so shocked they couldn't rest in peace for a year afterward."

"You miss your family, don't you?" Leda picked up a book and glanced at its title before setting it on the pile of papers in the book shelf.

"I had fun as a kid," Sharon said. "Dad worked hard at the gas station, but we had a big comfortable house. And all those brothers came in handy when I reached the dating age." She took Leda's coat and hung it over a dress in her closet. "You know."

"No, as a matter of fact, I don't," Leda said.

Sharon remained half inside the closet while the awkward pause between them hung round her shoulders. She listened to Leda puffing up the pillows and straightening the linen on the couch.

But she could not hide forever. When she came out, Leda was lying in the flood of a table lamp, a manuscript propped on her belly. Without questioning her, Sharon went to the cupboard and brought back two clean glasses, filling each from the bottle lying half empty against a slipper. Then she sat down beside Leda and handed her one of the glasses.

"You're quite a little Miss Fix-It, aren't you?" Leda said, moving the rim of the glass along pencil marks on the paper.

"You have to feel that you're doing something for the salary." She tilted her glass to her lips and swallowed half of the contents, glad for the burning warmth.

Leda set her glass on the rug.

"You don't want anything?" Sharon said, allowing the question to hang naked between them. Then, moved by the same reckless confidence that had flashed through her in Leda's house, she reached for the manuscript.

"You don't want me to read it?" Leda said.

"Not now." The urgency in her body came alive in the two words. For a second, she felt Leda holding onto the pages. Only a moment. They glided, then, released to her.

Sharon set them down beside the glass. The glare of the lamp searched out the single line of care beginning to eat into Leda's complexion. Sharon tilted the lampshade, softening into shadows the oval contours, the golden curling lashes with their questioning golden eyebrows.

"You know what I want," Sharon said. The desire raging through her made the words rough.

But Leda's hands grasped her shoulders. "You're lying to yourself, baby," she said, her words slow but firm. "You're lost and unhappy and you feel guilty about me."

"That lousy bastard," Sharon said, her mind snapping back to Ralph and to Jay simultaneously. A surge of strength filled her and she tore free of Leda's hold.

"Sharon, listen to me."

"I don't want to listen," she choked. "What's there to listen to, anyway?"

"Please."

Sharon swallowed hard, tightening her throat around the tears beginning to form there. "Don't try to make excuses for me, Leda. I can't see why you insist on thinking I'm such a kid."

"I didn't say anything like that." Leda's finger touched her cheek and moved down to the top of her lip, resting there.

"No, but you imply it with every move," Sharon said, leaning away from the touch. "Do I manage, somehow, to look like a virgin to you? With my history? With underwear draped all over your apartment? With guys throwing me around like a...a...I don't know what?"

Leda sat up on one elbow. "Relax, baby, and stop trying to feed me this hard sell about your sex life."

"Then what is it, Leda? Why do you keep evading me?"

And there it was, finally, ejected from the core of Sharon's being, the desire spoken, crystallized, waiting for fulfillment. She did not search now to find this answer in Leda's eyes or in Leda's mind. Sharon was past listening. Already, the whiskey churned through her. She could not see beyond the lithe body waiting for her touch, the compact breasts widely spaced and resilient. "I need you," Sharon whispered. "Don't you care at all?"

The urgency in her words was not so much a question as a command. She felt the force inside her growing, moving toward Leda, craving the contact of skin and warm breath, needing the strength and circle of arms around her back, the touch of lips along her throat, the forgetfulness of passion.

"Sharon..."

But Sharon could not wait to listen. She pressed her lips down, covering Leda's open mouth with her own. Her tongue darted forward, thrusting to find contact. Twisting around, she moved her body on top of Leda's, feeling the concave stomach, the length of thigh. She felt Leda squirming beneath her.

"You must," Sharon croaked against Leda's mouth. "Please."

Her lips travelled along Leda's throat to her ear. Forcibly she held her down to the bed, sensing the rapid breathing, the beating of Leda's pulse, knowing the leap of desire arcing to meet her own.

And, slowly, as she kissed her, she felt the gradual response of Leda's body. Then Leda's arms came tight around her back. They clung together, pressed tightly into each other's curves, silent yet wildly alive in the first blue streaks of dawn.

Secure in her conquest, Sharon turned onto her side, bringing Leda onto one hip. With trembling hands she sought and found the zipper of her slacks. And she shivered, remembering the sleeping body against her that afternoon.

"I could love you," Sharon whispered as her fingers crept along the smooth underthings, probing the curve and dent of flesh.

But Leda did not answer her. Nor did Sharon expect an answer. She knew herself to be one of dozens in and out of Leda's life. It didn't matter. Tomorrow was anybody's guess. But tonight, Leda lay here, beside her. Sharon pulled at the sweater, wriggling it up till her fingers found and unhooked the satin brassiere. She darted her head down to the nipples, finding them soft and hardening them rapidly with her lips. Sharon's thoughts whirled past recognition as her mouth moved without restraint over soft, yielding flesh, the curves of throat and arms, the hollow of secret, fragrant places waiting, mysteriously, for her touch.

And yet Leda did more than wait. Vaguely, Sharon felt the responsive movement of hands and mouth, the entwining of legs to hold her in the grip of tight thighs. Struggling to keep her senses alert, Sharon remained aware of every nuance, every breath and turn from Leda. Love seemed to reach out and cup her, to hold her high, carefully, above pain and knowledge of shame. She floated luxuriously on a rich carpet of desire, protected forever from remembrance of brutality. As she floated, Sharon gave and gave of herself, pouring her love and her craving for love as though into a brimming cup.

She clung and arched and gave again... and yet again. Faintly, she felt a fingernail digging into her side. And she smiled with the final knowledge of shared surcease.

Afterward, they lay on the narrow couch, watching the light spreading around and over their naked bodies.

Sharon closed her eyes and snuggled in against the side of Leda's breasts, inhaling the faint odor of perspiration that mingled with the lilac perfume. Her mind lay pleasantly blank. Blue and cloudless. If she could only lie still, here, like this, all trouble would cease to exist.

"You know," she said against Leda's flesh, "I feel completely at peace with everybody."

She felt Leda's hand stroking the braids which had fallen from their pins and come loose.

"Isn't that nice?" Sharon continued.

"Very."

The sound of Leda's voice jogged Sharon back to reality. Suddenly she became aware that this was Monday morning. A thrill of anger charged along her spine. In protest, she flung an arm across Leda's waist and tried to pull her closer.

"You're going to be happy, too," she said irritably. "I'll see to it."

"Good. Now go to sleep for awhile."

"But I don't want to sleep." And as she said it, Sharon pulled herself up. "I don't want to sleep away our chances."

"Chances for what?"

"Chances to live a second life," she said.

"Yes," Leda said with patience. "I know you have a fetish about youth. That's why I can't understand what you're doing with me."

The mockery again, flaunted like a protecting armor. Sharon twisted around and kissed her on the nose. "I'm going to spoon feed you from the fountain of youth," she said and let the giggle inside her bubble up.

But Leda did not join in the merriment.

"Can't you ever listen to me?" Sharon urged. "I know you think there's no point in running away. And the first time you told me, I almost agreed with you." She took a half smoked stub and lit it. "Only, now I've changed my mind. Really," she handed the stub to Leda, "I don't see what difference it makes what you do. Ralph'll think the worst anyway."

"True," Leda said bitterly.

"I don't know how many scenes like last night you've had to put up with."

Leda shrugged and mashed out the butt again. Sharon saw the energy, the suppressed anger, the frustration.

"Plenty of them, I'll bet," Sharon continued, encouraged to make her point. "Plenty, and still he hasn't done anything about taking your boys away from you. I mean, taking custody and all that." She folded her legs and grasped the ankles. "You know why, don't you, Leda? It's as obvious as day."

"If you're going to give me the routine about money..."

"All right, I won't give you any routine. I only want you to be happy. You believe that, don't you?"

For once, Sharon felt that she was telling the truth. Yesterday she had wanted to use Leda for a nursemaid. But today, she wanted to share with her whatever they might be able to find of contentment together.

"Yes, I believe you," Leda said quietly.

"And I'm not trying to make you do anything in the heat of emotion. That's obvious too, isn't it? I mean, we're sitting here, calm as two card players, aren't we?"

Leda's mouth pursed in amusement. "Looks more like strip poker, at the moment."

"I'm not joking now, Leda. Will you please listen?"

"I'm listening."

Sharon took Leda's hand off her thigh and held it still. "Well, my point is a very simple one."

"That we go to your folks in Old Overshoe."

Sharon's eyes flashed irritation. "You insist on making it sound so foolish. And I think it's the best thing in the world for both of us. Ralph won't find us, I guarantee that. It'll just be for a few weeks till you've pulled yourself together."

"Till who's pulled together?"

Sharon flushed, but said nothing.

"But why your hometown, anyway?" Leda said. "The way you've been harping on it, it must be something pretty special."

"But we've gone through all this, Leda. I told you how nice and comfortable it is and ..."

Leda sighed and reached out to pat Sharon's hand. "Take it easy," she said. "I understand."

"Understand what?"

Leda shrugged.

"I don't understand you," Sharon said.

"So much the better."

Sharon swung off the couch and marched around the room, needing something to do with her annoyance, finding nothing. "You puzzle me beyond endurance."

"Do I, baby?"

"And stop calling me baby. Everything I say, you twist into nonsense. Is that fair?"

"Well, maybe not." Leda sat up and pulled the sheet to cover her legs. "But I'll tell you this: if it makes you happy to go home, we'll go home. As you said, I've nothing more to lose anyway."

Leda's words rolled toward her like so many Christmas presents. Sharon felt herself brightening as though she were transparent. She ran across the room and flung herself across Leda. At last she had the one precious gift. The gift that could help her really to forget, to build new and stronger tissue over the wounds of her past. The gift of time, of distance, of love.

The threat of Monday morning, the impending meeting with Jay dissolved. "I love you. I do love you," she cried against Leda's neck.

"We won't take anything," Leda said, in an odd voice. "We'll go right away."

CHAPTER NINE

They made three stops before leaving town. One at Leda's bank. One at the house for Leda's car. And one at the gas station because the Jag ate oil.

Sharon spread the map on her knees and rolled down the window, letting the wind at her hair, feeling it cleanse along her scalp, blow away the clogged and dragging past. She had turned Jay off like a radio. And she searched Leda's face, willing her to turn Ralph off in the same way. Without speaking, she watched the steadily held profile, the splay of tan leather gloves along the wheel, the green reflection of sun glasses along Leda's pale cheek.

Abruptly Sharon folded the map and pushed it into the glove compartment. "I probably know the way by heart," she said. "It was the longest, nastiest, most apprehensive bus ride in my life," she added, recalling the crisp telegram from Jay permitting her to come to New York.

"First time away from home?" Leda said.

"Yes." Sharon leaned back and gazed out at the tips of trees displaying their leaves to a golden sun. "I must not be very unique. You seem to know it all so thoroughly."

"You'll know it all too," Leda smiled. "Just wait."

Sharon didn't want to know it all, but she didn't say so. One thing in particular she didn't want to know was whether Jay would be so hard up for an editor that he would try to trace her. She shivered. It would be just like Jay to run her into the ends of the earth.

But so long as she was at home, what could he do?

The length of her relaxed into satisfied pleasure. She had managed the perfect barricade.

"What are you grinning about?" Leda said, glancing at Sharon with a flicker of curiosity.

"I thought you were watching the road," Sharon answered and leaned her head against Leda's arm. "Some driver." She yawned and continued to smile, knowing that Leda would not press the subject. A pleasant stability had begun to settle inside Sharon. "When are we stopping for lunch?" she murmured dreamily.

"Not for two hours, at least. I want to get well on the way before we make any stops."

"Two hours?" Instinctively, Sharon's glance moved to the speedometer. But maybe Leda always drove this fast on the Thruway. Sharon felt her senses snapping to attention and she sat up straight now, her mind filling with new questions. Quietly, she watched the sprawl of road ahead of them, empty on their side, going upstate. And then, seemingly for no reason, she turned and peered through the back window, searching for ... For what?

"We'll stop and pick up some sandwiches," Leda said.

"It's all right," Sharon answered, trying to resume a casual manner. "I'm not on demand feeding."

"And a couple of containers of coffee," Leda continued as though she hadn't heard.

As she spoke, Leda swerved and the car skittered across the gravel drive to a log cabin diner.

"I'll be back in a second."

Before Sharon could reply, the door opened and slammed shut. She watched Leda stride between two parked trucks and disappear.

Sharon clamped her teeth together and leaned over to study the dashboard for a knob that would turn on the radio. It was silly to fuss over Leda's behavior. Probably just a case of nerves. And everyone had a right to suffer from nerves once in a while, Sharon told herself, remembering the dizzy weekend she'd just gone through.

She could not find the radio and instead, pulled out the cigarette lighter. The taste of tobacco on an empty stomach sent a twist of pain that subsided into vague nausea. A sandwich wouldn't help much. She needed something warm to drink, something milky and soothing inside.

Impulsively, she swung out of the car and followed Leda's path between the trucks.

The long, narrow shack smelled of bacon grease. At the far end of the counter, Leda stood at the cash register. Sharon passed a group of men huddled over their coffee and reached Leda as she was putting bills into her raincoat pocket.

"Hi," she said, touching Leda's elbow. "I decided to have some pancakes." She slid onto a stool and called her order.

Without turning, she could feel sparks of anger bristling beside her.

"Take your time," Leda said, leaning against the stool beside her. The paper bag crumpled in her fingers. She set it down beside the napkin holder. One hand folded into a fist for a second, then relaxed, the pink nails splayed helplessly. "I'll be in the car."

Sharon heard the door bang shut. But it was childish, this apprehension. Whatever Leda might be thinking, there was no actual reason for worry. What could Ralph do to either of them?

Sharon forced the pancakes down her dry throat, spooning herself courage while she ate.

When she came back to the car, Leda had the motor idling in a low, urgent pitch. Sharon had barely closed the door when the car lurched backward and swung onto the asphalt again, slamming her against the door handle.

"Hey," she said on a note of strained laughter.

But the grimness around Leda's tight lips increased. "I didn't know you made a habit of needling people," she said.

The car spurted forward as though responding in galloping good humor. Sharon remained quiet, puzzled by Leda's shifting moods, uneasily aware of her own desire to goad Leda into

revealing the depths of herself. But they had twelve hours of driving before they reached Maine. Plenty of time to get back on solid
ground.

The day blossomed. Houses and farms sped by, unfurling
a countryside of peace and open living. Sharon gazed out at
the long rows of new cabbage, the dark, fertile earth rolling
away into velvet hills. The world seemed so real and moist and
fragrant out there. Her own problems a figment of somebody
else's mind. Space and calm filtered in among the jumble of
her thoughts. She didn't want to argue or needle Leda. Enough
room for everyone stretched around them and inside herself.
She thought back to the breakfast incident and realized it had
been spite on her part, a crazy willfulness, a need to strike out
at whatever she could not understand. Just one more habit from
her years with Jay.

She watched the sun begin to curve toward the horizon, bur-
nishing the distant slopes with wide strokes of orange. They had
been driving steadily through the tense atmosphere of their mis-
understanding. Clay colored dust powdered the windshield and
she felt it gritty on her teeth.

"You must be tired," Sharon said, realizing they had not spoken for almost three hours.

"I'm used to this," Leda said around the cigarette butt which
hung dead and black from between her lips. A wisp of curl lay
flattened to her temple, blown there by the steady gust from the
open wing window.

"We're not going to get there tonight, anyway," Sharon persisted in a mild tone. She reached up and took the stub away,
lighting a fresh one from the almost emptied package.

Leda took it, but held it between her fingers on the wheel.
"Maybe," she said. "But we're damn well going to try."

Sharon's eyelids burned from fatigue, yet she strained forward eagerly as they drove down Lynbrook's main street at last.

The town lay silent beneath a three-quarter moon. An occasional store light burned dimly. At one in the morning, even the drifters had curled in somewhere. Awnings flapped in shadow.

"Let's park," Sharon said. "I want to walk around."

"You'll walk in the morning," Leda said. "Where do we find the nearest bed?"

But Sharon had come vibrantly alive, her nerves perking to the tune of memories that echoed in the sight of Lenny's drug store, the Feed and Seed Shop, the rows of darkened windows above the stores.

"There's a motel three miles out on the north side. But can't we park for just a little minute?"

"No."

The firmness shut Sharon up. She felt the surge of taut temper as Leda floored the gas pedal. They roared loudly through the sleeping streets and for the moment Sharon felt grateful that they were arriving at night when no one would see and have a chance to judge the change in her.

Tomorrow morning, all would be smoothness and smiles, she felt sure. A warm bath, a good night's rest, and a delightful manner would return to both of them.

They drew up at a green neon light blinking *Clover Court* in silent rhythm with the sound of crickets. Sharon stretched her arms in the brisk air and inhaled the fragrance of distant pine. Meekly, she followed Leda to the manager's office, trusting Fate not to confront her with one of the townspeople she knew.

A skinny man in army fatigues took the night's rent in advance and brought them to a center cabin.

Alone with Leda, Sharon flung herself face downward on the bed and stretched all the muscles she could find.

"I feel like a lion that's been let loose," she sighed against the pillow.

Behind her, Sharon heard the clink of metal hangers as Leda hung up her coat in the empty closet. Then the flicking of aluminum blinds closed out the world. She shut her eyes and waited, knowing Leda's irritations had begun to dissolve. That soon she would feel the weight of Leda's body beside her on the cotton spread. It did not matter how much they argued or that she did not understand the many moods sliding through Leda. Only tomorrow mattered. Tomorrow, in Lynbrook with people who knew and loved her. And as Sharon turned and moved closer in Leda's arms, it seemed, almost, as though tomorrow were already here.

She lay quite still, focusing on the caress of Leda's fingers along her sweater. Obediently, she lifted her hips, letting the slacks be drawn down. The unconscious, smooth knowledge in Leda's movements gave Sharon the feeling that her body was a package being opened. She could almost see the dozens of women on whom Leda had perfected her technique.

But it didn't matter. Nothing, nobody else could possibly matter as Sharon's legs widened to encircle the woman, to grip and hold her close.

"Love me," she whispered against Leda's mouth. And as she said the words, her nails dug into Leda's back, needing to tear the skin, to make her mark of possession.

Sharon felt stitches tear and Leda's bra strap gave way. The spread of soft flesh beneath the wool sweater pressed against her own breasts. Flames of desire leaped in her stomach, licking forth to encircle and devour the living thing in her arms. Thoughts of Lynbrook, of family, of contentment fled.

There would be only this moment, this need thrusting itself in the scented darkness.

"Easy, baby," Leda whispered.

Sharon felt warm fingers encircling her wrists, moving her arms.

"No," Sharon said hoarsely. "Let me."

She had never done this thing before. But the dizzying drive toward conquest urged her, strengthened her insistence. Leda murmured something, but Sharon felt the warm vapor only and did not hear the words. Yet she felt the sudden yielding of Leda's body as it moved beneath her.

"I need you," Sharon murmured to the warm flesh.

Leda's fingertips moved through her hair, grasping her scalp. "Go ahead then."

The cheap bed swayed with their bodies. A rustle of heavy foliage came through the windows to mingle its restlessness with Sharon's searching. As her lips sought Leda, the world seemed to splinter away in a million glistening points of desire ...

"Well?" Leda said into the ebb of silence that followed.

"What do you mean, well?" Sharon's nostrils prickled at the odor of fresh cigarette smoke that did not seem right in this country air.

"I mean, how did you like it?"

Sharon searched the voice for its usual signs of mockery. But the darkness seemed to have thrown a searching eye on Leda's feelings. And instead of ironic amusement, Sharon heard a strange touch of uncertainty.

"How does one put these things into words?" Sharon said, struggling for time to understand her own twinge of discomfort. She wanted to say: *laugh at me, damn you.* But she fell silent instead, her eyes focusing in the darkness on the ceiling fixture that hung down like a grotesque mammary gland. "I guess I'm too tired to think," she added, aware that Leda still listened.

Listened and would remain tuned in on her thoughts for the rest of the night. Sharon could feel the alert wakefulness and wondered what questions, what fears, what cravings drove this woman who could have everything in the world, it seemed, except happiness. Sharon reached across the crumpled blanket and patted Leda's thigh. "Why don't you get some sleep?" She had meant to sound affectionate. But the words hung disinterested, almost sharp between them.

"That's what I thought," Leda said.

"What do you mean?" Sharon turned on her side, away from Leda. "Or, if it's going to lead to another of our famous arguments, maybe you'd better not tell me."

"Yeah."

With a convulsion of impatience, Sharon sat up. "Now, what is all this hopeless mumbling?" Her words rang out in the dark with the sharpness of a fishwife's. "Am I supposed to analyze every move, every second of my life? You want me to lie here and dissect what we did together? For heaven's sake, Leda, what do you think I am?"

"I don't know, honey. What are you?"

For some reason that Sharon could not grasp, Leda's words cut through her. The desire to fight drained off, leaving Sharon empty. "What's that supposed to mean?" she said dully.

"Nothing," Leda said abruptly and turned over, pulling the blanket across her shoulder.

All desire for sleep faded as Sharon lay rigid with angry confusion. Questions, unceasing questions made a tangled rope that seemed to have tumbled her flat. What did Leda want that she had not given? Sharon's memory travelled along her bruised thighs and into her guts, aching still from the force of their love.

No, she had not stinted Leda on passion.

Sharon listened for the rhythm of Leda's breathing, wondering if she were really asleep.

"I don't like to fight with you," she said softly. "I want us to live together like intelligent people."

"Whatever that means," Leda murmured.

"It means," Sharon continued, hanging onto her patience, "agreeably, constructively, with plenty of good times."

Besides, why had Leda come along at all, if all she wanted to do was fight? The restless fear began to niggle inside Sharon as this question turned itself over. She must be doing something wrong. Something to alienate Leda. But if they continued to fight, the whole town would know it in a week. And if they became gossip, they would soon become something much, much uglier. One couldn't afford such a reputation. Not in Lynbrook.

Clearly, Sharon knew that she would have to give in to Leda's whims. Snuggling in close, she put her arm around Leda's waist and pressed her lips to the cool, naked shoulder blade. "I love you," she whispered.

And they both lay open-eyed and in silence until dawn.

The first noisy clattering of birds brought sleep that drifted across Sharon's mind with a veil of childhood memories. She saw again the tall red silo and smelled the pungent odor of horses on that far away day when she's smoked her first cigarette and first examined with a little boy the differences between them.

And in sleep, her arms tightened around Leda, pulling her body closer, preventing her from running away down the hill as she had watched that little boy run while she stood with her panties in her hand and his grandmother glowering in the doorway.

CHAPTER TEN

As Sharon awoke, her hand patted the empty mattress but found no touch of Leda's body. Her head jerked with a sudden rush of terror and bumped against the night table beside the pillow. Then she heard the sound of water running behind the closed door and the moment dissolved away into daytime.

Daytime?

Strong sunlight struggled in through the tightly closed slits at the window, only to be lost in the flood of lamplight. She slid off the bed and went to pull the blinds. But her hands stopped beside the drawstring as she realized her own nakedness. Not like living in a city apartment, high up where nobody saw you or cared if they did. One had to remember a million precautions that went with small town living. And, Sharon smiled to herself, she must have grown quite rusty about this matter of minding everyone's business.

She padded back to the bed, slipped her feet into the sandals and let herself into the bathroom.

Behind the shower curtains she could make out the shadow of Leda's body, the bend of elbow as she scrubbed along her ribs and around back.

"Can I join you?" she called above the water.

Leda's soapy hand pulled the curtain aside and Sharon stepped into a spray of steaming needles.

For awhile she stood, letting the water stream over her shoulders, contemplating the scene this would make to a Lynbrook audience. And yet, she thought, beginning to lather her belly, how harmless it really was. Two women, two bodies warm and wet and slippery, touching each other now and then in the closeness. Sharon took the white cloth and rubbed it over Leda's back, surveying the long red welts that her fingernails had brought alive. Her own body felt rested now and good. She stood quite still as Leda turned to face her and bent over, kissing each nipple hardened in the pour of clear hot water.

The half-smile in Leda's tenderness reassured Sharon that there would be no arguments this morning.

They dressed quickly and went out to the car, where Sharon waited while Leda returned the key.

"Where do we eat?" Leda said when she came back.

"Dozens of places," Sharon answered, waving her hand nonchalantly. "You can choose either of two drug stores."

It wasn't until the car bumped over a familiar rise in the road that Sharon felt the first true shock of being back home. In three minutes the car would veer left and idle down a series of five sharp turns. They raced past an old farm and Sharon's eyes searched out the particular, crooked oak she had known. And beyond it, the house with antiques where nobody bought anything except an occasional washtub. Excitement pulsed and pumped nostalgia thrillingly.

"Stay to the left," Sharon said. "It gets a little muddy where the asphalt is cracked away."

And Sharon grinned with pleasure as the dirt road appeared.

"A fast growing town," Leda murmured.

"They're just waiting for me to get back," Sharon said with a wink.

As they came around the final stretch, Sharon saw the cluster of houses and stores glinting like jewels. The town seemed to have frozen in place. Not a new piece of wood marred her recollection of home.

"Looks bigger in the daytime, wouldn't you say?" Sharon's voice trembled happily.

"Oh, very."

The Jag crept now in the traffic and Sharon strained to peer into the stores.

"Pull your head in, turtle," Leda said, "or it might go home in another car."

But Sharon hardly heard. Her mind leaped busily from one remembered experience to the next, reliving her whole childhood in the ten minutes it took to drive up and park in front of Lenny's drug store.

"I'll phone the old man," Sharon said, bounding out of the car. "Give him a chance to change his overalls for the honored guest." She wrinkled her nose at Leda's raised eyebrow and dashed ahead of her past the Revlon ad languishing between a display of gleaming white bed pans.

In the crowded store a flash of shyness touched her. She had hardly worn lipstick three years ago. Now she felt conscious of Leda's tight sports clothes stretched across her high breasts and molding the flanks of her behind. A moment's regret that she hadn't brought a valise of her own things hunched through her shoulders. Maybe she ought to wait before renewing old friendships.

But even as she thought this, Sharon knew that it was already too late.

A clatch of women at the soda fountain paused in their conversation. The moment's breathlessness told Sharon that she had been recognized. Recognized and classified. Deliberately, she stopped in her tracks and turned to smile at the wide-eyed, cool faces and watched the masks unbend stiffly into responding nods and hesitant smiles.

"Hi," she called to the boy behind the counter, remembering the angular face.

"Hi there, Sharie. You back?"

Sharon boomed a grin at him and thought what a bitch it was not remembering names. She would have to bone up.

In the phone booth she dialled the old number and pressed the receiver hard to her ear to keep it steady.

After the tenth ring, Sharon told herself how silly it was for her to expect Pop to be sitting indoors on a day like this one. Probably out back in the old rocking chair he kept on the lawn. Sharon came back into the store to see Leda buying cigarettes at the side counter. As she surveyed the tall body with its trim though wrinkled clothes and its short hair, Sharon realized how much the two of them together would stand out among the dowdy women who bought their things in the local dry goods store. She watched Leda and saw the image of herself. How much she must have grown in New York.

She motioned Leda to the soda fountain and ordered two dishes of scrambled eggs from the boy who was happy to see her.

When they had finished and stood out on the street, Leda said, "If those women were a sampling of small town good will …"

But Sharon took her arm and walked her to the car without answering. She didn't want to think about these unaccountables. They didn't fit into her plans.

She watched the roll of hills and spread of farmlands blend into the familiar countryside patterns of Spring, pointing out to Leda the homes of people she knew.

"Real friends," Sharon added, still needled by the experience in the drug store.

And then, beyond a pasture of white and brown cows, grazing beneath a low flying plane, Sharon saw the rambling, white-washed house, its dark roof still spattered with the stray red shingles her father had put in during the years.

"There," she said in a gasp.

Leda slowed and gazed over the wheel. "Looks comfortable."

"It is."

The front porch still lay out of view, but Sharon's gaze scanned to find the rocking chair and maybe her father in it, dreaming as he watched the hills come and go behind formations of cloud.

"Well, hurry," Sharon said, and the car spurted forward again.

Before Leda had pulled up the brake, Sharon sprinted out the door and around to the back yard. The lawn seemed particularly neat, she thought. No old bicycles, no dog. No rocking chair. Things had gone pretty much to pot when her mother had died. During ten years, she had become accustomed to what her father had termed, "loose living." Now it seemed strange, almost stiff to see neatness again. The first flush of zest began to dribble away, prodded on the move by curiosity.

She found Leda sitting on the wide green rail that surrounded the front porch. Glinting in the sunlight, obviously freshly painted. The gray wooden porch had been painted recently, too, and there were no chairs on it.

A flash of panic ran coldly through her. She strode to the curtained front door and rattled the knob with one hand and rang the bell with the other.

"Hey, take it easy," Leda called.

But the desperation in Sharon's thoughts leaped out of control.

A few minutes later, when the door opened, Sharon began to feel dizzy. She knew the woman who stood there. And she tried to tell herself that maybe her father had sold the house.

"How are you, Liz?" Sharon said. "Where's my father?" Her voice cracked on the word.

"Sharon Porter, of all the Lord's children." The woman's gaunt, square jaw bobbed mechanically. Her light blue eyes darted over Sharon's appearance. "Why don't you come on in?" Her pepper and salt hair floated up in whisps from the center part that divided her bony face into two halves of a granite block.

"Where's my father?" Sharon repeated.

The woman wiped her hands on a fold of her cotton print dress, pale as her eyes. "And bring along your friend," she said, hardly glancing at Leda.

Leda came off the rail to stand beside Sharon. "We're looking for Jared Porter," she said.

"Heard y'both the first time," Liz nodded.

Sharon felt Leda push her through the doorway and onto the oval braided rug that protected the slick wooden floor. A sweetish odor of cooking blueberries warmed the rooms.

Leda introduced herself and Sharon heard the words buzzing around her ears. She felt a convulsive need to reach out for the wrinkled throat and shake it till the head fell off.

"You don't have to worry about your father none," Liz said, bringing them into the large kitchen. "That is, if you are worryin'." She set out two white painted chairs from the oval table and motioned them to sit down. "Jed's doing right fine by now."

Sharon stood behind the chair, her palms pressing into the wooden edges. "That doesn't tell me where he is," she insisted, spitting the words hard at the large, straight-backed woman taking out a pie from the oven and setting it on the green and yellow squared oilcloth.

"No, I guess it don't," she said.

Sharon felt the flame of hate burning inside her, just as she had always hated this woman for the patiently sadistic manner that wore everyone down to her own way of thinking.

But if her father had sold the house, why hadn't he written it to her?"

"He'll be around about five-thirty or so," Liz said and poured coffee from an aluminum percolator into green mugs.

With this piece of information conceded, Sharon allowed herself to sit down. She felt the touch of Leda's knee beneath the table. A nudge meant to steady her temper, to bolster the sagging morale, to relieve the strain Sharon felt tearing at her insides.

Liz took a wide bladed knife and sectioned the pie, lifting the broad pieces quickly so that the blueberries remained inside the crust. "Supper's about six," she said. "How come you didn't think to let us know you were coming?"

Us.

"You doing Pop's housekeeping these days?" She felt the pressure of Leda's foot on her own, but it couldn't steady the growing fear.

"Cookin' *and* the cleanin'."

The triumph in Liz's stolid assertion ended all further questioning.

"Close on to two years this comin' July," Liz continued as she rested back beneath the pots hanging under a cuckoo clock.

Sharon's fingers closed around the handle of the mug but she knew she couldn't lift it to her lips without spilling the contents. She speared the section of pie and felt the tines sink into the plump berries.

"Take a bite," Leda said, nudging her arm visibly. "It's good. Better than store bought," she added.

Sharon stared through her, unhearing.

"I suppose you'll have lots of things to talk about with your father," Liz said. "Catch up on all the news."

Sharon's head began to move slowly from side to side, as though by telling herself *no,* she could erase this woman's presence. But even if the woman herself disappeared, the house reeked of her cleanliness, her domination. Nothing could wash her out. Something of her had seeped into the very pores of the house Sharon had once called home.

Haltingly, her gaze groped upward to the clock. Hardly noon yet. How could she live through the hours till her father returned? And when they did finally meet, what kind of change would she see in him? Sharon could just imagine the old guy, scrubbed down, groomed like the house. Subdued. If Liz had gotten that rocking chair out of the back yard, it meant that her father had given in. Or been broken in, like a wild horse. Her fingers felt cold around the hot mug. She wasn't sure that she could stand to see it.

"We keep a guest room," Liz said in the silence. "You can take your friend upstairs and freshen up."

Guest room. Sharon's old bedroom, probably.

"No," Sharon said, her voice dull. "There are things...I've got to do." She pushed the chair back, feeling its legs glide over the polished linoleum. "I'll come back."

Somehow, she managed to get up and remain steady on her feet. They led her back to the door while her body tingled as though the blood had been drained away. Sharon lurched toward the car, not turning to say good-bye, not wanting to see anything on either side of the gray automobile. She flopped onto the seat and waited for Leda, arms lying heavily in her lap, shoulders sagging. Her eyeballs seemed to grate inside the lids, as though trying to go blind.

Mercifully, the car veered and sped away. Her mind seemed to catch and hang onto the hum of the motor, rushing in flying, tiny circles without meaning.

They returned to the motel and Sharon sat in the reading chair beside the venetian blinds for almost an hour before the tears came.

"Why did he do it?" she said into space. "Why did he have to marry that one. Of all the women in town, why her? ..."

"Now, baby," Leda said from where she lay on her back. "You don't want to go asking why people marry other people, do you?"

Sharon clenched her fists and pressed the knuckles against the chair arms, wanting to hurt herself. "But, Leda, she's so terrible. You don't know."

"Maybe your father doesn't think so."

Leda's statement bounced away beyond Sharon's reach. "I don't expect you to understand."

"I know, I didn't grow up with her and all that. Well, kid, I'm sorry for you. But let's not forget he made a free choice." She reached for the package of cigarettes and peeled off the cellophane. "Anyway, what do you want to do about it?"

"I'd like to kill her, that's what."

"Um humm. But on the more practical side..."

"Don't make fun of me, Leda. Not now. Please."

Leda swung off the bed and came over to the chair. She leaned Sharon's head against her thigh and held her cheek in her warm palm. "I'm not making fun," she said. "I'm just trying to get it across that little tyrants like you have a tougher time than the rest of us. It's always such an uphill battle, trying to keep people in line, isn't it?"

Sharon closed her eyes and pressed her face harder into the wool roughness of Leda's slacks. "Is that what I am to you?"

"Let's face it, Sharon. You know you've got to boss everybody around or it's no go."

Sharon heard the words, but beneath them she heard the velvet acceptance, the kindness that forestalled any need to defend herself.

"Do I boss you?" Sharon said, her hand sliding gradually up the back of Leda's leg.

"Sly one."

"Well, do I?"

Leda caught the hand and held it still. "You wouldn't mind."

"But what's that got to do with my father?" The strength of her anger, of her humiliation dragged her back. Distinctly, she saw Liz again, all calm and self-satisfied in the doorway.

"There's not much you can do about your father, Sharon. Why don't you let it go?"

"And what instead?" Sharon's voice shook with its bitterness. "Let her think I've handed him over to her on a silver platter?"

"Tell me something, honey. Is he your father or your lover?"

Sharon wrenched away and stalked to the other side of the small room. She put her forehead to the pine wood wall. "You are impossible," she rasped. "Like Jay ... like Kermit ... like everyone else. You think you've got me classified as an A number one villain, or fool, I don't know. Well, I don't care what you think. That seems to be the way, doesn't it? Not to care what other people think?"

"Get hold of yourself." Leda said from across the room. "We've got an audience."

"I don't care about that, either."

"All right, baby. This is your town, not mine."

Sharon spread her hands flat to the wall. The confusion had begun to circle round her, spiralling inward, trapping her into fighting with Leda. But she couldn't just walk out, admit to defeat. Not again. Not after Jay. And besides, where could she go now? Where in the world was a place for her? A future? And love?

"I can't just turn my back on it," she said, struggling to lower her voice and control the energy of her desperation. "Are you going to stay with me?" she said, turning now to challenge Leda. "Or am I being too tyrannical?"

The word fascinated Sharon with its utter absurdity. A crooked smile played on one side of her mouth as she watched Leda take a comb from the back pocket of her slacks and run it slowly across her temples. If she could really be tyrannical, all her problems would be solved instantly. She wouldn't need to keep someone around all the time or run from Taft Publications as though Jay could have her arrested.

"Careful now," Leda said. "I can see what you're thinking."

The mockery again. And yet Sharon felt a twist of guilt. "My forehead's made of glass, I know," she said. "But why shouldn't I admit that I need you?"

"Simply because it's not so."

A splurge of laughter burst from Sharon. "How, in your mind, did I get to be all things strong and self-sufficient?" She watched Leda shrug away the question. "Now tell me," she continued. "Because if I could have your opinion of me, my life would be completely different."

Yet even as she asked, Sharon could see that Leda had no intention of pressing the matter further. Obviously Leda did not and could not share her curiosity. But it must all be a joke, Sharon thought. Leda's design to bolster her feelings or an indication of

Leda's faith that she would eventually straighten out the jumble of her life. And this demonstration of confidence quivered like an arrow in Sharon's heart.

Sharon felt a sudden flash of discomfort that made her unable to face Leda. Propelled by its impulse, she strode across the room and stepped out onto the porch, slamming the door tight between them.

Sharon strode onto the gravel and across the empty highway, wandering among the wide spread trees, moving in the crisp sunshine that seemed to touch all living things with contentment except herself.

Tyrannical. The word popped into her head again and she tried to thrust it away as a bad joke. It seemed to contrast pathetically with the river of frustration racing through her. But what if she could only pretend to be tyrannical? For an hour. At five-thirty, when her father came home. And just what might she accomplish?

She picked her way among a shower of daisies, then sat down on the grass, leaning her hands to the cool earth. To judge her old friends by today's series of misfortunes was hardly fair. Instead of getting morbid, why not try a little action?

Sharon's mind seemed to race along on the crest of a new expectation. There were so many girls with whom she had been close back in high school. Their faces came up vividly along with the shared secrets. She remembered the bathroom huddles, the discussions about who had gone how far with what boy. And what it felt like.

Some of these old friends would remember. Remember and understand. Surely they would not turn against her. They would help her to recapture her old self, get back on the path of decent living. Perhaps find yet the happiness she had hoped for with Jay.

And as she thought this, Sharon realized what she must do. Go back and begin over again. Go back to the old shed where she had first known the meaning of passion, the promise of adulthood. Live again those moments of innocence, of hope and trust.

When she came into the cabin room, she found Leda seated at the desk, scribbling on the back of a picture post card.

"All aired out?" she said as Sharon passed her.

"Practically."

She had intended to share her thoughts with Leda, but something stopped her now, demanding secrecy. "Can I mail that for you?" she continued with forced casualness, taking a lipstick and Leda's comb to the mirror.

"Just a note to the kids," she said.

The idea of Leda's family thrust itself like an intruder into Sharon's mind. She combed her hair out with vigorous strokes and rolled it into a tight chignon, telling herself that life, after all, did go on despite her troubles. Then she paused to stare at her wide, haggard-rimmed eyes, as though to search in them for the selfishness that she could not deny. In a burst of annoyance, she realized that she could not afford for Leda to desert her.

"Tell them you're having a ball," Sharon said, her voice icy.

"What in hell's the matter with *you?*"

But Sharon didn't dare answer truthfully. How could she tell Leda that this was no time to be thinking of anything that could separate them? That she was, yes, afraid of her kids. Afraid that they would intrude more and more. Shoehorn her right out of Leda's life. And that now, more than ever, she needed Leda, needed all of her.

"Just a little jumpy," Sharon said, smoothing a gloss over her words. "I need a long, fast drive by myself." She continued to fill in the red outline of her mouth. Her lips seemed larger today, wider, cushion-soft with voluptuousness. "Clear the cobwebs out of my scattered brains."

"You mean you want to take the car and leave me sitting here?" Leda's tone rose on a lilt of disbelief.

"Maybe half an hour or so," Sharon answered quickly, patting powder across the short length of nose.

"Not on your life," Leda said. "Not in Old Overshoe, you don't."

The threat of another argument lowered in the room. The senseless gripping of wills.

"Okay, forget it," Sharon breathed.

"What's going on in that brain of yours?" Leda said slowly, letting the pencil roll across the desk.

"I said, forget it."

But the frustration rolled up in Sharon, tantalizing as desire. The need to hit out at Leda for having money, for having self-possession, for having kids slithered through Sharon's thighs and upward, stroking her as though with long, pointed nails. "I said forget it," she repeated, talking, this time, to herself, unable to let go of the crazy tip-tilting desire that spread-eagled through her groin.

"Why do you want the car?" Leda persisted, her eyebrows even, her features calm, only the pale lips moving enough to speak.

"A whim," Sharon said and tossed the lipstick onto the bed.

"You're lying."

The matter-of-factness slapped Sharon harder than needling accusation.

"My glass forehead again," she said, trying to imitate Leda's style of mockery. "But then again, why would you dare trust a tyrant?"

"Sharon..."

The single word seemed to plead for good sense.

"Don't you realize that I've got to see my old friends again," Sharon blurted. "I've got to find out for myself that it isn't all like...like my father. Or those women in the drug store," she went on breathlessly. "I've got to know I'm still worth something to someone here. Can't you understand that?"

"Is that it?" Leda said. "Really it?"

"Yes, I swear it." Yet even through her sincerity, Sharon felt the discomfort of something that she could not quite touch.

"All right," Leda said. "I'll believe you." She tossed the car keys beside Sharon's lipstick on the bed. "Go."

CHAPTER ELEVEN

Sharon's toe eased the gas pedal down to the floor. She felt the motor's surge of power beneath her will and it transfused strength into her. She gripped the wheel and leaned forward. Her body felt like an arrow whistling toward its destination.

No thoughts of old school friends crossed her mind now. The speed of travel cleared away these excuses. How could she care what had become of them? Married, most likely. Country-fat and self-centered. They would not be able to help her, she knew.

As her mind evolved this clearly, her arms turned the wheel. The car squealed away onto a dirt road and bounced through pits and over small rocks, following the winding path that led beside the creek.

Reaching the top of the slope, she could see beyond the field of high, bending weeds to the silo. In the full sunshine, its red paint seemed faded to patches of pink and maroon, reminding her of dried blood.

Sharon pulled up the handbrake before a barbed wire fence that marked the road's end. The path to the silo lay overgrown in tangled weeds and coarse grass. She pressed her spine hard against the bucket seat and said aloud: *What did you expect, kid?*

But the urge to relive it forced her out of the car at last.

She crouched and slithered beneath the wiring and started across through the grasses that whispered around her calves, winding sometimes around her leg like dozens of hands trying to hold her back. The sunshine warmed through the wool of her sweater. She felt cold perspiration rising to meet it.

Past the silo, she could make out the farm house chimney and the back attic windows, both newly bricked. Whoever lived there made a home without farming. modern day Lynbrook, she thought. A town strangely unreal to her.

Her breath came rapidly as she fought her way past the silo to the old shed and pushed at the door. Its rusty lock clanked against the wood. Curls of paint fluttered onto her arm. She walked around it twice, only to find that all the loose planks had been boarded over. No way in, unless she pried loose the rusty hinges behind the padlock.

Crazily, her nails began to dig at the screws. Then she pried at them with a car key until they jiggled loose.

All thoughts of time and place disappeared as a frenzy of terror and desire snapped her back fifteen years. She shoved the tilted door backwards and it gave beneath her force, slogging backward into damp shadow. The pungent odor of hay spread through her. Sharon stepped inside and breathed of it deeply. She listened for the scuttling of mice along the floor. Nothing but silence and emptiness.

She walked around through this silence, retracing her steps as she circled, smiling, yet shivering with a vague apprehension.

"Hey there, you!"

The voice that called with such possession and demanding raced toward her from the farm house. There would have been plenty of warning, plenty of time to put on her underwear and run, she thought, if only his grandmother had called to them that day.

Her feet began, even now, to tingle with the urge to run. The years' old guilt and humiliation flamed alive. She could almost watch it bursting again from its original seeds of surprise. But she held herself steady. Insane to run now. And run from what? The memory of a child's growth into knowledge? No. No one, no matter how desperate, could really run away from that.

Nervously Sharon felt through her pockets for a package of cigarettes but found only a rumpled Kleenex.

How damned silly, she told herself over and over again. But the jumpy feeling refused to settle.

Whoever he was, she could almost feel him pounding toward her, cutting angrily through the unkempt grounds, cursing her for making him take such trouble. She started to go toward the entrance, then checked her steps. There would be some slight advantage in seeing him clearly before he recognized her. Let him squint through the shadows while he yelled.

Sharon jammed her hands into the pockets of the slacks and pressed her fingertips against her thighs. What would Leda think when she found out all the lies?

Yet the thought of Leda dissolved before the more pressing need of the moment. And as the man appeared in the doorway, his short, stocky outline sharp against its background of sun, Sharon felt her body cringing deeper into the shadows.

"Who's in here?" Without stepping across the threshold, he leaned forward, a thatch of brownish hair falling sideways down to a thick eyebrow.

Sharon remained silent. The leathery, pointed face seemed to jab toward her while one freckled arm hung onto the door frame. The rolled up sleeve of his denim work shirt flapped toward the elbow. All of him seemed as unkept as the fields.

"What're you hiding for?" he continued. "You got to come out sooner or later. Better come now."

"I suppose so," Sharon called and felt a smirk of joy as he recoiled in surprise.

"A woman?" he breathed as though to himself and stepped now onto the blackened floorboards.

Sharon heard the creaking and felt a twinge of regret that she had started this. "You don't know me," she said quickly. "I was just driving through..." The sentence died as she recalled that she could not reveal her motives.

"Just driving through and decided to break into somebody's property." He was coming directly toward her. "I don't know about where you come from," he said, "but we don't do this sort of thing around here, lady. We use the comfort stations that are right and proper."

Sharon felt a flush of warmth spread down from her forehead. "No," she shook her head violently. "You don't understand."

"I don't, eh?"

"No," she repeated, smelling now the perspiration of his clothes. "No, you don't. I'm Jared Porter's daughter. Sharon." Her voice lilted hopefully. He would understand and let her go. Whoever he was, he wouldn't press anything against one of the townspeople.

"Who?" he said.

"Sharie Porter. You know the Esso Station on Mill Street, across from Gumpie's Dry Goods?"

She could feel him straining to see her better. "Jed Porter?"

"That's right," she encouraged. "I used to come around here quite a bit when I was a kid. And I sort of couldn't help myself before. You know, thinking about old times."

"Sharie Porter," he repeated, musing on the name.

"I guess maybe we knew each other?" she said, beginning to edge around him.

"Guess maybe we did." His drawl squirmed snakelike around her. "I'm Kublick," he said softly. "You remember Eugene Kublick?"

Eugene.

The name sparked through her. She could hear again his grandmother shouting after him as he disappeared down the hill. "So you're Eugene," Sharon repeated stiffly.

"The very same."

Sharon wanted to fill in the silence that seemed to leer at her. Cross out the memory that must be floating over his eyes.

"We never did get a chance to see much of each other," he continued. "I guess I was scared to death of that old hen. She's been dead some many years. And you? Whatever became of you, little Sharie Porter?"

"Let's go out in the sun," she said, "so I can see you better."

"Oh, I can see you very well right here," he said softly. "I can see you, little and smooth as day."

She knew what he was thinking and despite herself, the skin began to prickle along her belly. The curiosity of her innocence blended with the knowledge of experience. Vividly, she saw again his tiny maleness, its helpless yearning.

"Weren't we happy kids?" Eugene said.

She felt the tentative touch of his fingers along the inside of her arm.

"No worries … no inhibitions …" he drawled. "And I was free as a bird then. Do anything I wanted to without having to answer to anyone who couldn't run as fast."

Sharon stood frozen, yet bathed in the strangely golden liquid of nostalgia.

"I guess you finally got married?"

"No," Sharon said.

"No? No one man big enough, eh?"

The insinuation clutched at Sharon's groin. It seemed to tear her secrets loose and spread them before the world's dirty eyes.

"More fun being kids," he breathed near her cheek. "Isn't that the truth?"

"I think we ought to go outside," she said hoarsely.

"You seemed to like it well enough in here … once."

"Don't embarrass me, Eugene."

"I didn't mean any such thing. I only wanted to remember the fine times. Isn't often that a man has a chance to relive his youth, you know. Not with three wild kids and a loudmouth wife hammering away at him. But I don't suppose you know that kind of trouble. Anyway, I guess you came here to remember what we used to do here and I don't see the reason for hiding it from your old friend and partner."

His sudden and unexpected earnestness sliced out Sharon's hesitation. "That's true enough," she said. "You know, Eugene, I got caught doing something wrong I didn't know was wrong."

"And I guess you haven't been caught since," he chuckled. "Like the rabbits and the deer," he said softly. "Uncanny smart enough to stay hidden during hunting season." He drew a long breath. "This sure is a big surprise to me, Sharie Porter. I can't think of any nicer thing I would have wanted to have happen to me."

The exaggeration of it touched Sharon with a feeling of closeness to him. It seemed hardly a second ago that they were innocent children together, forced into knowledge by the harsh intrusion of an adult world in which they did not belong.

"You know something, Eugene?" Sharon said softly. "I used to think about you very often. What became of you, who you married."

As she spoke, Sharon felt him tugging at her wrist, the way he used to. Automatically, her legs folded and she sat down cross-legged beside him among the warm whisps of hay.

"Remember the Indian stories I used to make up?" he said lightly.

"Scared me half to death with those wild medicine men. What was his name?"

"You mean Igu Buck-buck."

"Yes," Sharon laughed. "Old Igu and the flaming mountain." She heard him shuffle around to face her.

And then their knees touched, ever so gently. Almost as though by accident. Yet she knew it was no accident at all.

"Then one time, I asked you why girls had to squat when they..."

"Yes," she interrupted him quickly.

"And you said you didn't know," he persisted. "You said I should look and find out."

"Because I didn't know how boys could manage it standing up," Sharon said, keeping her voice impersonal.

"And we thought it would be a good idea to compare for differences." As he spoke, his hand darted out and caught her flatly. Bluntly.

Sharon sat quite still. Too late to protect herself. Too late to move away. Weakness began to tremble through her body. The heel of his hand began to massage up and down.

"I remember how you moved yourself in closer to me," he said, his voice quiet and level, "so I could get a good lesson."

Sharon's mouth went dry and her thighs closed on his arm.

"You don't have to worry," he whispered. "Gramma's dead and in the ground. There's no one to stop us," his voice was exultant. "No one."

She felt herself sinking backward to the floor. The insistent hand seemed to know all her secrets as it circled slowly, rhythmically. He slid up beside her and pushed her own hand downward. "Go ahead," he urged. "Be curious again."

And her fingers began to move with a desire free of her brain's fear. As she held him, she wriggled in closer, her hips lifting and thrusting. She felt his hand tugging awkwardly at her slacks and paused long enough to help him.

Pieces of hay jabbed into her naked behind, but she hardly felt them.

"Eugene," she said against the point of his shirt collar. The name conjured up all her lost youth and innocence and all the strident desire that had finally come to flower in her matured body.

His rough hands pinched and pulled at her, finding her nipples to squeeze them till they became twin points of pain.

The odor of stale tobacco from his teeth prickled pungently at her nostrils and she moved closer to grasp and hold him, to fulfill at last the promise of her lost innocence.

Sharon felt the plunge and thrust of his need. Her arms lashed out wildly, then folded round him, muttering his name over and over like a dirty word in which she had taken final, forbidden freedom.

Her flanks battered against the creaking wood as she gave herself up to the need of engulfing him within her. The touch of his hair against her lips, the thickening chest pressing her ribs seemed all an extension of her own desire and her hands slipped swiftly along his back, down his hips as though she could hold this craving in her hand long enough to squeeze and crush it lifeless.

Then her thighs jerked suddenly together and she held him in the very point of her convulsion till it faded away into drowsy surcease.

From the distance to which he had crawled, she heard him say, "Little Sharie Porter."

But as she watched him fixing his trousers, she knew he was speaking of someone they had both just killed.

CHAPTER TWELVE

The sun had slipped halfway toward the horizon by the time she got back to the car.

Sharon sat behind the wheel, weak and numb and without thought. She stared at the warped fence, the rusted barbed wire gradually crumbling through the years of changing seasons. Was her life to be a dead end like this, too, with no past, no present and a hopeless future?

She twisted the rear view mirror and blinked at the slice of her face reflecting lassitude. The smeared lipstick made a shapeless orange blob beneath drawn cheeks. The yellow brown eyes seemed to have receded behind the heavy lids.

It was all too obvious what she had been doing.

Idly, she picked a bit of hay clinging to her elbow and dropped it out the window. Leda would know she had lied. Nor could she think of any way to explain it.

She started the car and turned it slowly around in the narrow, rutted space, driving carefully down to the highway.

What she had done would draw the line irrevocably between them. Leda would be lost to her forever. She couldn't blame anyone for kicking her out after this afternoon's episode.

Yet she couldn't have helped herself. There was nothing in it premeditated. Or even desirable. The whole thing had been revolting.

But why should Leda understand this when she hardly understood it herself? She could still smell the odor of hay rising from her clothing. Her stomach twisted in revulsion.

As Sharon drove, she patted at her hair, thinking only of the hot, hot shower she would take. Scald her skin in the cleansing vapor. Let the memory of it go up in steam.

Sharon kept her gaze steadily on the road while she drove through the center of Lynbrook. Subtle pangs of betrayal seemed to emanate from the lines of stores, the buildings and people which had not, on the surface, changed. But changed they had, truly. Changed cruelly and without warning to her.

She sped through and onward to the motel. Better to face Leda's forthright anger, her open disappointment than be knifed in the back by a town that pretended to be loyal.

The scraggly dog still lay on the gravel and Sharon steered around him to pull up in front of the cabin. Its door stood ajar and she raced inside, thankful to be back.

"Leda?" she called and noted simultaneously that the room stood empty.

She bounded out and around to the back lawn. Leda reclined in an orange and green striped sun chair, hands locked behind her head, eyes closed to the sun which glinted in silver lights from her newly washed hair.

"Leda," Sharon repeated, coming up to her and throwing the shadow of herself across Leda's face.

"Hi," Leda said without opening her eyes.

Sharon had heard the relief in her own voice and knew that Leda wouldn't have to probe far to know everything. Yet for once, she felt willing for Leda to know it all. Maybe, in the telling of it, Sharon could begin to understand the fierce thing that drove her.

"I'm back," she said.

"Obviously."

"But, Leda, I'm *back*."

"Well, stop insisting or I won't believe you," Leda drawled, the mockery beginning slyly.

Sharon plunked herself down on the wide arm of Leda's chair. She wished she could pry Leda's eyes open. If only the woman would look at her and see it all and understand and forgive her. In a steep wave of desire, Sharon needed forgiveness just as desperately as she had needed to do the thing for which she wished this forgiveness.

"Leda, please," she said.

"I know," Leda persisted. "It's time for lunch."

With a sigh, Sharon stood up again. "I'm going to take a shower," she said flatly. "Maybe then you'll see fit to open your eyes."

She watched Leda lower one of her hands from behind her head and search the air for hers.

"No," Sharon said. "Don't touch me. I don't want you to touch me now."

"So be it."

The three words seemed to sum it all up for Sharon. "I don't know what you want me to do," she said. "I feel so damn lousy I can't even think straight."

"Go take your bath first," Leda said. "And if the hysterics prove to be really necessary, we'll have them after a good lunch."

Sharon began to back away from the indestructible calm that had risen in front of Leda. "Why won't you let me reach you?" she whispered.

"Why, indeed?" Leda's mockery twinkled brash and secure.

Sharon turned now and fled for the cabin and the hot water in which she wished she could drown herself.

She stood directly beneath the shower head and let the water beat down onto her skull. The pounding, insisting force seemed to batter against her brain, making a mash of it to wash down the drain. As the water slid over her face, she could see him again, his hot eyes knowing her, the heel of his palm finding her. Incredible that she had wanted it. And she saw that, too. Her own craving that had risen to meet his. Every bit as eager.

Sharon pressed the soap between her legs where he had touched her. She wished it would burn. Burn and dissolve away the tiny machine that hummed along without her knowledge or control. Sex had been invented, not for pleasure, but to destroy the weak. The survival of the fittest. And it was sex that weeded out the unfit.

Two years ago she would have laughed at such an idea. Even one year ago. Maybe even last month. But she could no longer evade a growing knowledge.

It wasn't Jay who had ruined her life. No, Jay had nothing to do with it, except as the unwitting accomplice.

Yes, she had ruined her own life. And all by herself. She had ruined it with desire. Consumed her chance for happiness in the flames of her craving.

The truth scalded through her and she turned the water on even hotter, watching her skin growing pinker around the breasts. Yet, even in the moment of this shame, she watched her nipples shiver and grow hard, as though defying her to ignore the body that possessed her life.

"Come on in there."

"In a minute," she called back, glad to be able to say something aloud to prove her actual presence in the midst of this sudden nightmare descending on her head.

She swung the faucets off and stood dripping in the heat and heavy vapor. How odd to come suddenly awake at the old age of twenty-three. What heights of stupidity had kept her so blind all these years?

Sharon stepped out onto the soggy bathmat, depleted of all energy. She lowered the toilet lid and sat down, tightening for an instant against the cold touch of the plastic. She stared down at her toes, wrinkled from so much water. The same feet, the same legs, the same knees she had always known. Only there, beneath the triangle of dark hair, lay the secret. She wondered if Leda knew it. If Kermit knew it. If Jay had known it. Surely Jay had known.

Knuckles rapped lightly on the door.

"Let's get this show on the road," Leda said.

But Sharon heard no impatience and she sighed, finding it difficult to lift an arm, to take the towel, to begin the lengthy process of blotting up the thousands of droplets clinging to her skin and all its crevices.

Her bra, as she put it on, felt damp across the band and gave off the acrid odor of perspiration. Whatever cleanliness she might have felt from the bath became soiled again, contaminated once more with the recollection.

But finally, she got into her things, brushing off what she could of dirt and straw that still clung to the back of her slacks and sweater.

"Well," slowpoke," Leda said, surveying her as she came back into the room. "That's a little better, though, isn't it?"

"What's better?" Sharon said, needing to say something, to find the sore and open it.

"Not your mood, certainly," Leda smiled. "Anyway, look at these nice pink cheeks I'm growing. Maybe even get my tan back."

Sharon studied the light manner and knew that Leda intended to continue evading a showdown. She sat down on the edge of the mattress and leaned back, holding her elbows stiff, thrusting her breasts upward. "I don't want to go for any lunch," Sharon said in deliberate, steady words.

"All right. You stay here and I'll go."

"But I don't want you to go either."

Leda remained at the door, holding it open with fingers that grasped the edge of it tightly. "If I don't get something inside," she said and tilted her head around the curl of cigarette smoke, "I'll be much too weak to face ol' ax-face Liz."

Sharon felt her insides close in a jolt of anger. "Don't worry about that," she said from between stiff lips. "We're not going back."

"But we have to."

"Why?"

"Because she's going to tell your father. And he'll be looking forward to seeing you."

"I doubt it," Sharon replied in a wave of bitterness. "I doubt that very much."

"Well, I don't." She took the cigarette and flipped it out the door. "Anyway, stop arguing so much. You're making a chain smoker out of me and if there's anything I can't stand in a person, it's addiction."

"Leda, stop kidding, will you?"

"Kidding, me?" The slow smile which Sharon had seen that first night darkened her eyes again into deep, dark pools. "What on earth have I got to kid about?"

Sharon held her words, feeling them pile up in her throat.

"Now, come along like a good child and we'll have some of Lynbrook's finest."

"I mean it, Leda. You won't take me seriously today, but I'm telling you the God's honest truth." She sat up straight now and clasped her cold hands tightly in her lap. "I have no intention of going back there."

"We drive all this distance and you change your mind because of..."

"Because of why doesn't have to make sense, does it?" She took a deep breath and held it for a moment.

"Granted, life isn't a course in Aristotelian logic," Leda smiled. "But it's rather nice to rein in the whims now and then, don't you think?"

"Yes. Starting tomorrow. I promise you, Leda." She stood up and went to the woman, pushing the door closed and resting her arms on Leda's shoulders. "I've caused you an awful lot of trouble and I'm selfish enough to have my own way this time." She began to draw Leda toward her. "Can't we just turn around and go back to New York? Or out West? Or to India? I don't care. Only please, take me away from here before I lose my mind."

Sharon's hands moved up to cradle the back of Leda's head.

"What has a lovely, shrewd, talented young thing like you got to lose her mind about? Dear old Lizzie?"

As Sharon saw Leda's eyes narrowing in amusement, she knew that there was no use trying to be clever.

"I'm not so shrewd at all," Sharon said on a sigh. "Nor talented, nor lovely. I don't even think I'm very young any more."

"Well, it's all a matter for comparison, isn't it? But just the same, I think you owe it to your father to see him. So long as we got this far..."

"No, I'm not going, Leda, and that's all there is to it."

Sharon's voice rang out and seemed to bounce back at her.

"I guess you mean it," Leda said quietly.

"Can't you see I mean it? I mean, you're a smart woman and all that. Why are you giving me a hard time about...almost nothing?"

"Nothing?"

"I don't like the way you repeat me."

"So you don't like it."

Sharon felt the challenge in Leda beginning to rise. And in response she could feel herself slipping away, backing down. But she couldn't back down, she couldn't permit herself to be a slave to the nameless fears, the nameless cravings that directed her. Whatever the penalty, whatever the suffering, she had to learn to control these little tyrants inside her. Or wind up in Hell.

"Leda, you've got to understand something," Sharon began again, patiently. "I'm going to get my way this time. I can't face my father. What's more, I don't want to face him. I want to leave and start all over again."

"Start what all over?"

"My life, if that doesn't sound too dramatic. Until today, I've been chasing ghosts. I thought my life was here. But I caught up with one of those ghosts today. And believe me, the revelation hasn't been very pleasant."

As Sharon spoke, she heard in her voice a first glimmer of sincerity. The sound was strange and wonderful to her ears as she realized that she was speaking, not to make Leda do her bidding, but out of the freedom of honesty.

She took her hands from Leda's shoulders and moved them back to her sides. "You've been very good to me," she said. "But I have no right touching you. Not now."

"And what does that mean?"

Sharon listened to the different facets in Leda's voice coming up to the light like a many sided crystal. "It means I think you deserve a hell of a lot better than some confused dope who's using you like a life preserver."

"I appreciate the advice," Leda said, taking Sharon's hands and putting them back on her shoulders. "But try to remember, please, that one confused dope in any two-some is plenty."

"You puzzle me, Leda, you really do. Here I am, finding for the first time in my life the guts to tell someone to run from this self-seeking bitch and that someone deliberately closes her eyes. What's the use of honesty if it doesn't change things?"

She felt Leda step in closer and her hands move along her back. "Why don't you just spit it all out? You know, it made me sick at heart to hear that car squeal off like a wild animal this afternoon."

"You want it all?" Sharon said, feeling the first thrill of anticipation. "And when you get it ..."

"Let me worry about that."

Sharon nodded and pulled herself free. The moment had come and she felt like a bull she had once seen in the ring in Mexico. Only she was more than the bull, she was her own *torero,* about to kill forever the unscrupulous personality that had been living inside her without permission.

She sat down on the bed and made Leda lie with her head on her lap. It would be easier to talk, to tell all the truth, if she could feel Leda's response as she stroked her temples.

Haltingly, Sharon told it all, from the beginning, how it had been when she was a child and up through what had happened this morning. The words seemed carved out of fire and they seared her tongue as she forced them out into the air.

Yet each sentence seemed to purge her, bleeding the strange demon of its strength. She spoke and she felt the relief of confession, wringing clean every shameful moment of its hold on her.

Finally, with parched throat, Sharon concluded. It had not taken long to tell and yet she felt stretched across the span of a thousand, pain-ridden years.

"So," Leda said, sitting up again. "You'd like to believe this is the end of things?"

"No," Sharon mused thoughtfully. "I'd rather think it is the beginning. Of something maybe a little more decent in my life."

And she smiled calmly at Leda now, knowing for the first time that the only true answer she would ever find would rise at last from the dark well of her own experience.

CHAPTER THIRTEEN

Sharon's calm, yet persistent urging finally convinced Leda. Nor did Sharon's mind turn nostalgically to say farewell to Lynbrook, as the car swung out onto the highway toward New York. This time, Sharon had no room for memories. Her thoughts were too busy working out how she would conduct her first meeting with Jay.

Alternatives rose and died. Sharon twisted in her seat as though wrestling physically with the dilemma.

"You got ants?" Leda said as Sharon recrossed her legs and leaned an elbow on the window ledge.

"It should only be that simple," Sharon mused. "I've got all these good intentions, but no brains to work them out." She stared sightlessly at the trees whipping past. A swell of disappointment lifted and crashed into the hopes so neatly stacked for the future.

"Any of us could say that." Leda hung a cigarette at the corner of her mouth and let it dangle there unlit. "Take me, for instance," she continued and the cigarette bobbed. "Thirty-five and still running around like the proverbial beheaded chicken."

"It's all my fault," Sharon said quickly. "I shouldn't have tried to drag you off like this."

"Please," Leda smiled. "Don't try to take the responsibility for my life, too. I knew before we left that this was a merry-go-round we were riding. But I needed the change of pace, you see. Little distractions in the over-all pattern of things…"

"Make life bearable," Sharon concluded for her.

Leda nodded.

The speedometer lifted gradually to sixty five and Sharon gave herself up to the gulf of time before them. She leaned back and tried to sleep. But tiny nodes of anticipation jiggled like bumps on the asphalt, jouncing her into wakefulness.

"I ought to see Ralph with you," Sharon said. "And help you explain."

"What for, you dope?" Leda gave her a quick glance that sparkled. "He's not your problem."

"True," Sharon said. "Yet somehow, I feel…I don't know what I feel, Leda. But with his temper. And these circumstances. I get the feeling that you never have left him quite so flat. So suddenly. Leda, if he's anything like Jay, I want to be with you."

Sharon could almost hear the pulse of her own anxiety thudding through the car.

"Gee, are you a morbid one," Leda grinned.

But the lighthearted manner did not reassure Sharon. The facts seemed to poke through the calm of Leda's poise, sharp and deadly. No manner of joking could clear away the fury with which Ralph would greet them.

"I don't care what you say." Sharon took away the cigarette, lit it and replaced it in Leda's mouth. "I'm scared of them. Both of them."

Leda exhaled smoke and the wind whisked it out through Sharon's window. "Come along, baby."

"I mean it."

"Of course you mean it. But you exaggerate."

Sharon rolled the window up past the level of her eyes yet the wind still felt too cold, prickling the skin along her arms. Somehow, Leda's flippant manner could not reassure her. Her words seemed to ring hollow, like false coins.

"Maybe you'd like to stay at my place for a while," Sharon said.

"No, honey," Leda responded, too quick with her enthusiasm. "Let's not make a soap opera out of this."

Sharon felt the force of Leda's determination and decided to let the subject drop. "I guess you know by now what's best," Sharon said, more to console herself than to concede the point.

As the car nosed along, Sharon could feel them hurtling dead-center into destruction. And yet, what choice had either one of them?

The odor of soot and exhaust fumes, the harried muddle of traffic, the press of tenements blotting out the sky announced New York to them early that same evening.

While they waited for a red light to change, Sharon turned to examine Leda, wanting to absorb every angle of her body, to impress the image and feeling of her forever on her brain.

"What are you staring at?" Leda said. The irritability of fatigue seemed to gnaw around the question.

"Nothing," Sharon whispered. "Nothing at all." Deliberately she turned her glance to her own cuticles, examining them with seeming casualness. "Come back to my place with me," she said easily. "Just for a few minutes."

"What for?"

Sharon heard no harshness in the question, only the directness of reality.

"I want to say good-bye to you," Sharon said. "Properly."

In answer, the Jag swerved through Central Park and headed west to the one way avenue that went directly downtown.

They had to search for a parking place, then walk three blocks to Sharon's house. A clumsy silence had grown up between them and Sharon felt herself straining for words to make casual conversation. The pointed fear kept rising in unexpected places, needling while it hovered over them both. Yet she could speak nothing of this to Leda. They had agreed, tacitly, not to mention the future. When it came to pass, each would deal with it in her own way.

Sharon felt the shock of seeing the old apartment house, standing in shadow between the street lamps. Had she expected it to go away during her absence? Had she really expected huge changes in the seventy two hours of her absence?

But somehow she no longer belonged to this routine of struggle against impossible odds. The garbage cans in the hall, the naked bulbs, the aroma of boiling onions—none of these things touched her now. She lived in this house only as a transient. There were other worlds more congenial. And somehow, she would manage to find her way to them. She believed now that she had found the strength, the incentive to make something of her life.

Sharon picked her way through the jumble of papers and snapped on a lamp.

"Don't look at it," she whispered into Leda's ear. "It's all a mirage."

She grasped Leda's waist and drew the woman's body in close to her own.

"What's all this for?" Leda said, stiffening and pulling back.

"Because I want to," Sharon murmured. "I want to remember something personal and good between us. With no taint of my selfishness on it."

As she spoke, Sharon's lips grazed along the soft neck and up behind Leda's ear.

"I want this one moment in time," Sharon whispered, "before the world falls in on us."

But she did not try to force Leda's response. Instead, she poised her fingertips lightly on Leda's back, waiting for the first hint of accession.

"Will you?" Sharon said.

Without answering, Leda moved out of the circle of her arms and went to snap off the lamp.

They moved toward each other and their bodies lowered to the couch. Silently, they began to undress each other, moving off sweaters and slacks, undoing bras, slipping off panties. The lifting of hips, the twisting of arms and shoulders occurred easily, without hurry, as the contemplation of desire mixed languidly with the taste of each passing second.

In the apartment beneath, strident voices of argument arose. But the flying barbs of dissension only served to draw Sharon closer to the precious warmth and acceptance between them now.

"I love you," she murmured against the curve of Leda's breast. And as she said this, she felt the pangs of sincerity isolated from the bursting passion in her flesh.

The tip of Sharon's tongue made circular trails along the lithe curves, resting now and then on the hardness of a nipple or the soft rise of Leda's belly. Her fingers held the insides of Leda's thighs, magnetizing them with tremulous desire. She felt Leda's legs close on her wrists and her hand wriggled upward.

Then Leda rose and forced Sharon back, pinning her to the couch with the pressure of her warm length. Breasts and ribs and stomachs seemed to melt one into the other. Sharon's teeth bit into her own lips and she clung to the woman as though swinging from the precipice of desire. The darting tongue flicked along her skin, paving its way toward fulfillment.

Sharon groaned into the darkness and her head spun dizzily. Her body seemed to fling itself into space as she felt the warm contact. Her teeth ground together, trying to cage off the rising scream of exquisite torture.

From her window, Sharon watched Leda crossing the street. The length of her slim body threw a long, ebbing silhouette as she passed beneath the street lamp. She saw the woman hesitate before turning the corner. But she did not stop or wave or so much as turn for an instant.

And Sharon knew it was best this way.

She drew the shade and came back to switch on the lamp. The electric clock lying on its side, patched together with band aids, heroically told Sharon it was three a. m.

In less than six hours, she would be facing the daylight... and Jay.

Knowing that sleep would be impossible for the rest of the night, she began gathering the manuscripts that needed reading. Then she looked up the phone number of a junk man and noted it down to call in the morning. It would be impossible to salvage anything from this apartment. And there was really nothing she wanted to save.

Sharon puffed up the pillows and settled herself to read from the stack of articles that had been waiting too long. Tomorrow she would get in touch with Jay and give him the ones that were publishable.

That was one way of getting started again on her life.

She lay out a fistful of sharpened pencils and dug her attention into the print.

Sharon had gone through only the first of three stacks when daylight began to seep around the edges of the window shade. As she glanced across the room, she felt the beginning stiffness in her neck and smiled, realizing that she had grown unaccustomed to long hours of work.

For a few minutes, she put a hot cloth to her shoulder. But then, impatient, she washed and dressed, needing to get out of the apartment and back into the stream of life. She would call the junk man from Jay's office. She had too much to do to spend precious moments in waiting.

As Sharon became part of the crowd gathering toward the subway entrance, she sensed the pleasant crutches of moral support around her. One needed a purpose in life. Even Leda, with all her money, suffered from the weight of aimlessness.

She thought of Leda and began to wonder what had happened last night with Ralph. Perhaps Leda would call eventually and tell her that everything was all right.

Yet even as she told herself this, Sharon knew that it would not happen. The story between them had come to a permanent close. By this time next week, perhaps Leda would have drifted into another adventure.

To worry about her was foolishness. She could handle Ralph, certainly. Apparently she had been doing so for years. And if she couldn't …. Well, there was little that Sharon could do to help.

Shrugging herself free from these depressing thoughts, Sharon moved with the tide down the steps and into the hot congestion of the subway. With the action of habit, she bought a week's worth of tokens and slipped them into the plastic container on her key chain.

In the train, she grabbed for a strap and hung on as the train rattled and squealed. She felt again the sway of bodies, the passing pressures that might have been deliberate though one could never be sure. Mechanically her gaze roved along the garish strip of ads, her thoughts leaping monkey-like from one inconsequential promise to another. She dared not think of Leda and she could not anticipate Jay. Here, in the hot, crowded train, she dangled alone in limbo.

CHAPTER FOURTEEN

Sharon swung through the glass doors and flounced across the plush gray carpeting to her office as though her world were right side up with all the little pieces precisely in their little places.

She smiled hello to the receptionist and proceeded down the narrow corridor flanked with cubby holes till she reached her own, with two small pots of cactus on the desk flanking a gold-framed calendar that Jay had bought her once to remind her of the importance of schedules. She swung around and into the swivel chair, plopping the manuscripts on the blotter and pressing her cold hands together in an effort to steady herself before seeing Jay.

With taut, dry lips, she smiled good morning at the secretaries and file clerks straggling past her. No one seemed aware of her absence. The great upheaval that had taken place this weekend seemed well hidden from curious eyes.

But certainly Jay must know it.

She stared for awhile at the black numerals on the calendar, wondering if she were out of step with time in this race for self-possession. Could she make Jay believe all the changes that had happened? Could she make him respect her enough to let her walk out of here with her chin up?

The clacking of typewriters from down the hall told her that nine o'clock had arrived. He wouldn't be in for another hour, most likely. Give her time to clean the things out of her desk drawers. Her life, it seemed, had become one great big act of disposal and for one brief flash, Sharon wished she could throw herself away with the trash.

She emptied bits of newspaper into the waste basket, tore up outdated memos and copied publication schedules onto a single sheet of activities. The flurry of activity flared and then died. When she peered outside at the wall clock, only fifteen minutes had gone by.

She phoned the junk man and told him to be at her house at two o'clock. She wrote memos to be returned with the more promising manuscripts. She swung around in the swivel chair some more and felt the last fragments of her calm skitter away.

Sharon had gotten up to go to the ladies' room for the second time when she ran smack into Jay outside her office.

They stood and looked at each other, Sharon stiff with the reflex of her uncertainty. She could almost see his eyebrows bristling.

"Good morning," she said, and heard it echo ridiculously.

She saw the small muscle on his cheek jump. Then he pushed around her and strode off down the corridor. Sharon watched him step inside his office. She heard the door slam and felt its jolt.

So.

This morning he was hating her. Hating her for lousing up the office routine. Maybe he had another editor already.

Impossible. Good ones weren't hanging around to be plucked like oranges in Florida.

He hated her because she had deserted him and left him helpless. That must be it.

Sharon leaned one shoulder against the wall and contemplated the gold letters of his name glowering back at her. A crazy sort of courage began to perk. The courage of clarity because, for once, she could see the thing against which she was fighting.

Returning to her office, she gathered up the stack of manuscripts and headed for her first showdown.

On a bet with herself, Sharon opened the door wide without knocking.

Jay stood at the window, his back to her, leaning on the sill with stiffened arms. She could see the wide triangle of his back pulling the jacket tight. For a second her heart leaped. She wanted to run to him and lean her head against his side. Run to him and apologize and ask him to take her back. To take her back on any terms.

Then the feelings dissolved and she felt herself burning with the fire of her new courage.

"I brought you these," she said, and dropped the manuscripts between the folders on his desk. A snapshot of her stuck out from his blotter. An old, cracked picture when she had worn her hair loose above the undeveloped body. "They're all ready to go," she added.

"Fine," he said. "Now clear the hell out. Who needs you?"

With a sinking feeling, Sharon realized from his positive manner that he had found himself another editor. "No one," she said quietly.

She heard the faint ring of defiance in her tone and stepped back, as though away from her own surprising words. "And who needs you either?" she added feeling a surge of mounting anger. "Who needs a self-centered animal that rapes and steals and hoards?"

"What?"

He turned and she saw the bloom of incredulousness alight in his dark eyes.

"That's right," she continued. "Little mousy speaks up. Only I'm not a mouse and I never really was one. I've strung along with you for three years. In good faith."

As though she had not spoken, Jay took off his jacket, hung it on the coat tree and began to roll up his shirtsleeves. Then he sat down at the desk and began to leaf through the manuscripts.

"I told you," he said, without looking up, "you're no longer needed here."

Sharon could feel him struggling to keep his temper. Was it going to be this easy? Was he just going to let her walk out forever without wanting to understand the thing that had caused this split between them? Didn't he care at all?

Maybe he never had, really.

A well of emptiness opened inside her. She felt cheated and lost and used up.

"You don't want to hear me out," she said.

"No."

"Not as an editor and not as a person." She felt herself clinging to a frayed rope.

"I've hired another editor," he said impersonally. "And as far as I'm concerned, you're not much of a person."

"Because I ran out on you, you think."

"Drop it, Sharon."

She saw the irritation wrinkling his forehead and knew that his pride had risen to overrun them. He could not afford to be interested. He had never come to her with questions. Only with commands. And, certainly, he wasn't about to start now. Especially not now.

"Who's your new editor?" Sharon said, wresting away from their argument to settle on more neutral ground.

"You know him," Jay said, his lips hardly moving. "You know him quite intimately, I've been told."

"Kermit Drake?" Sharon said.

"So it is true, isn't it?" Jay's mouth twisted into a smirk. "And I thought maybe someone was pulling my leg."

"No, it's true," Sharon said quietly. "Probably every miserable thing you've heard is true."

"Well, I've got the message by now." He turned and lifted the receiver, calling downstairs for containers of coffee. "You want out?" he said as he jabbed the phone back down again. "So you've got it."

Sharon remained speechless. She had expected a knock-down, drag-out fight from him. But there was nothing. Nothing except her own desperate need to face the truth and have him face it with her.

"Jay," she began slowly, "is this the way it's going to end between us?"

"Why not? Abrupt. Clean. What the hell did you come in for today, anyway?" He pulled open his tie knot. "Post-mortems? Well, I'm lousy at pulling the wings off butterflies. As far as I'm concerned, the end came when you took off with that buddy of yours."

"You know everything, don't you?"

"I know that you're a flip head."

"Not the sweet little girl you thought. Not the one on that picture, am I?" Her voice rose in bitterness. "Well, who do you think killed her, Jay Taft?"

"I'm not interested."

"What are you interested in?" Sharon waved a stiff hand. "Besides your money and your night life?"

"Sharon, I'm not going to have any female hysterics in this office."

The words, their level tone, cut the legs out from under her. "All right, Jay," she said quietly. "I just wanted you to know that I didn't leave without pulling all the ends together."

Without waiting for him to answer, Sharon plunged out of the room, swallowing the surge of tears.

Back in her own office, she closed the door and leaned her forehead down on her folded arms. She had anticipated every move he could make, every attempt to beat her back into sub-mission. Why hadn't it occurred to her that he could toss her out along with the useless memos? She had counted on his pride ... but not to work in reverse.

Sharon heard a quiet knock and the door cracked open, revealing to her blurred sight the impeccable pin stripe suit, gray bow tie and sleek blonde head.

"The clan gathers," Kermit said. "Welcome home."

"What's so welcome about it?" Sharon muttered, blinking swollen eyelids.

Kermit smoothed a stray hair on his temple and extended a silver cigarette case. "What's welcome?" He sat down on the edge of Sharon's desk. "Peace was beginning to threaten our happy family," he said. "That's what."

"Not with your big mouth flapping wide open all over the place," Sharon said, blowing her nose in a Kleenex from the bottom drawer.

"Oh, don't praise me for the actions of others. I am blind, deaf and dumb, didn't you know?"

Sharon pushed away the cigarette case. "All I know is Jay has a diary on me, detailed for every second. And now I'm consigned to rot with the rest of the rats in the galley. Thank you for the welcome home, but this isn't my idea of a warm reception."

"Oh, come, you know better than to blame me."

"Then how'd you get this job so fast? It only pays a hundred and a quarter a week. He didn't advertise it on a Times Square billboard." Sharon pressed her knuckles to her lips, fighting to keep up the mask of flip mockery she had learned from Leda.

Kermit inhaled deeply and exhaled smoke toward the pale green ceiling. "The details are pathetically simple."

"No doubt."

"But can't we talk about it over breakfast? I got up too late even for a quick aspirin."

"Let me tell you this, Kermit," Sharon said, mustering a smile, "if you plan to walk around this office like a chief executive, forget it."

"Oh, I don't plan anything of the sort," Kermit swung the cigarette grandly. "I only took this silly job as a fill-in till you got back. You know, stay on the good side of the guy who sends the checks. I have, after all, a fine appreciation of Jay Taft's ability to butter my bread. And other than sleeping with the guy, I'd probably do most anything to keep him happy."

"Well, I'm not back."

"But you are. I see you with my own two eyes."

"It's a snare and a delusion, Kermit." Sharon stuffed the Kleenex into her purse. "He just kicked me out. Really."

"Of course he did." Kermit took her elbow and led her out the door. "That's the knight's gambit."

They rode down the fifteen flights in an empty elevator. Sharon observed the bland mannered person beside her, wondering if his profession was writing articles or buttering up the people who bought them. And yet, Kermit seemed to have forgotten his own residue of ill-will toward her. Whatever his motives, she thanked him silently for this overt gesture of friendship.

Outside, they strolled across the street and into a busy Schrafft's. She had hardly eaten all day yesterday and nothing yet today. Perhaps the despair she was feeling had something to do with her empty stomach.

Despite her lack of appetite, Sharon ordered griddle cakes and bacon and set to work consuming it with methodical determination.

"You don't really want to hear the inside dirt, do you, Sharon?" Kermit sipped at a cup of coffee and set it lightly back into its saucer.

"Maybe not," Sharon said. "Anyway, what good would it do me? What future reference will I need it for?" Sharon cut another triangle of pancakes and pushed it around through the thick, golden syrup. "I'm convinced there's no future for me at Taft Publications." She managed to smile when she said it.

"Then what will you do?"

"I honestly don't know yet, Kermit. This thing has thrown me right on my little old noggin. Maybe I'll just crawl away and lick my wounds for the time being."

"To come back and fight another day?"

Sharon looked up at him and grinned openly. "Yes, how did you know?"

"I sort of know you. A little."

Sharon averted her flushed cheeks to her own coffee cup.

The junk man came half an hour late, but Sharon was glad for the extra time to gather all the odd bits into cartons.

She sat down on the edge of the couch and wiped soot from her forehead with the torn shirtsleeve. He was a bent little man with bulging forearms on which Sharon could trace the veins. She watched him lift the dead weights and swing them out the door, feeling as though with each carton he was carrying away another of her burdens.

An impulse to help, to hurry him up kept her tense. She went into the kitchen and inspected for the tenth time the empty shelves.

"That about does it," he said at last.

Sharon paid him, then closed the door to stand in the center of her emptiness. For once, she could spread her arms without knocking anything over. She could walk without picking her way over obstacles.

So it was done. And now what? What did it solve?

Sharon couldn't put it into words, yet she could feel an overwhelming sense of release from the distractions of her past. As she swung around in the room, her world seemed all full of shiny tomorrows.

When the phone rang, it resounded almost frighteningly from the bare walls.

The strange male voice held authority and education. Sharon was not surprised when he told her that Leda Michaels had authorized him as her counsel in divorce proceedings.

Yes, of course she would be willing to have an interview with him. Anytime. Yes, she knew both the defendant *and* her husband. Not well, no. But well enough. This afternoon would be fine, say around five-thirty?

Sharon held her breath as she hung up the phone. Every inch of her seemed to anticipate the torture, the disgrace, the drawn out humiliation that lay ahead for all of them. Ralph would certainly make the business as ugly as he could.

As Sharon washed and groomed herself with care, she tried to anticipate how she was possibly going to be of use to Leda. She could be witness, after all, to only the shabbiest part of Leda's life with Ralph.

CHAPTER FIFTEEN

The towering gray building on Court Street loomed silent, almost ominous as Sharon's heels clicked too loudly across the marble lobby.

A relief elevator man standing beside a stool with his newspaper folded on it rode her upstairs. Strangely, she felt as though she were sneaking in through someone's back door, coming here at this hour and with this mission. And then, with a shiver, she recalled that as a witness, she would probably be within earshot of Leda's deepest secrets. She felt no doubt that Ralph would strip the skin clean from Leda in his fury to find some fragment of revenge. The futility and the sadness of it washed through her. As though Leda had ever really enjoyed herself!

When Sharon saw Leda in the waiting room, it seemed to her that a hundred years might have passed since their last moments together. The flair of mockery had fallen like a curtain stripped from her naked body. She sat in a green plastic chair staring across at the back of the receptionist's desk. A line had etched lengthwise between her eyebrows. Her face seemed brittle and about to shatter into many pieces of despair.

A few seconds passed before Leda looked up and saw her. "I'm sorry we had to call on you," she said and stood up.

Sharon took the gloved hand and felt its iciness even through the tan cotton material. She wore a dark brown suit that hung loosely as though she had lost a great deal of weight.

"I'm glad to help if I can," Sharon said and sat down beside her. "Anything."

Ordinarily, Leda would have grinned and made a caustic joke. Now she merely resumed her gazing into a great distance that seemed filled with endless, futile wandering.

Sharon held back the many questions that leaped to her lips.

"He's going to wring us dry," Leda said. "You know that, don't you?"

"Let's wait and hear what your lawyer has to say," Sharon answered, finding no other way to avoid agreement.

"I've already spoken with him. This morning. It seems that Ralph didn't waste any time. I guess he thought he'd beat me to the punch."

"You mean, he expected you would be coming back for a divorce?"

Leda sighed. "Crazy, isn't it?"

"He must have been frightened out of his mind. Or maybe all the years of imagining things backed up on him this time." She took off her own gloves and pulled them through the leather loop on the side of her purse. "Poor man."

"Don't you bother feeling sorry for him," Leda said. "Until after you hear what Mr. Donovan has to say."

"All right," Sharon said, unable to hide the dread creeping into her struggle to maintain good spirits.

They waited now in silence until the receptionist flicked off the intercom, nodded to them to go inside and began putting on her hat.

From Mr. Donovan's corner windows, Sharon could see the indigo pattern of skyscrapers burnished in the final rays of the afternoon sun. Of all the millions crowded into the city, she wondered who would change places with Leda Michaels now. Who would take her money, her possessions, her sophistication, her contacts in almost every social circle?

"Sit down, ladies," Mr. Donovan said from beneath a graying mustache.

The courtesy of his speech made Sharon smile inwardly. When was the last time someone had referred to her as a lady? Her glance flickered over the slight figure buttoned into a charcoal gray vest from which dangled a Phi Beta Kappa key.

"Miss Porter," he folded small white hands on the cleared desk top, "I'm sure you can anticipate the questions I'll have to ask you."

Sharon felt his round-eyed gaze piercing her. "Yes," she said quietly. She shifted uncomfortably, wondering why Leda had confidence in this man.

Mr. Donovan cleared his throat. "Then let's start from the beginning."

Nervously, Sharon glanced at Leda.

"Go on, tell him," Leda mumbled. "Better here than on the stand."

"That's right, Miss Porter," his voice intruded smoothly. "We don't want to be caught unaware, do we?"

And so Sharon began to describe her meeting with Leda and their trip to Maine. As she talked, she continued to watch the scrubbed, aging face that twitched its mustache; and something about the quality of the attentiveness made Sharon withhold. Occasionally, he would interrupt her to make her explain the details of an intimate moment that she had shared with Leda. But Sharon struggled not to commit Leda to its guilt. The story took only brief minutes. Excluding the commentary of her own feelings, she could almost manage to gloss over the superficial story. Almost keep it decent, from Leda's point of view.

Mr. Donovan sat motionless except for the manicured fingers that clasped and unclasped as she spoke. As she watched his thick ring twinkling its square-cut diamond, Sharon kept thinking: *He doesn't want to help... He doesn't really want to help...* And finally, the whole story had been dragged out of her.

"Is that everything you can remember?" Mr. Donovan leaned forward as though to peer into the recesses of her brain.

"Yes," Sharon said firmly. "Everything."

"Why don't you let her go now?" Leda said in a voice hardly audible.

Mr. Donovan stood up and came around to rest his hands on Leda's shoulder. "You can both go now," he said. "I'll phone you later on, Leda. Maybe tomorrow. It takes a while to see how these things shape up."

Sharon followed Leda out.

The evening air had chilled the edges of the day, adding a bleak note to the promise of Spring.

"I don't like that man," Sharon said bluntly. "I wouldn't trust him as far as I could kick my own grandmother."

"Don't worry about that," Leda said, lighting a cigarette and drawing the smoke deep into her lungs. "He's a tenth cousin or something. I've known him for years."

"I don't care if you've known him since Adam."

"Well, it's a pretty cut and dried case, no matter who handles it."

The desolation in Leda's voice stopped Sharon's protest.

"I get to thinking about all the witnesses Ralph'll have trouping up to vouch for his parental and moral purity..." Leda stopped beside a bench and rested her handbag on the concrete arm.

"And all you've got is me," Sharon concluded for her.

"That's not what I meant."

"Well, if it's all that bad, why don't you try for a settlement?"

"Don't you think I've thought of that?" Leda flung her cigarette on the ground. "He wants it all. Every grimy inch. He wants to sit there in court and puff out the self-righteous chest. He wants revenge, Sharon. That ought to be easy to understand. After all these years of licking around me ..."

Unable to control herself, Sharon shuddered.

"And this sex bit absolutely clinches it. He can take the kids away from me forever."

"But, Leda," Sharon grasped her arm, "he's got to prove it. You read the newspapers. He's got to have pictures or something else tangible. He can't just leap up there and tell a string of stories." She sat Leda onto the bench and bent over her. "You know something, Leda?"

"Hmm?"

"I think he's bluffing."

"But, honey," Leda said patiently. "He doesn't have to bluff. Ralph's got it all on his side."

Yet all the way home in Leda's car and alone again in her apartment, the thought persisted, buzzing around Sharon's brain, distracting her. She bought a newspaper and scanned the classified ads for another job and another apartment. And even while she read, she kept seeing Ralph's face and Mr. Donovan's face. The two seemed to make a congenial pair.

Sharon slept only fitfully that night on the sagging cot. In the empty room, her thoughts seemed to grow and expand. Job hunting would fill her day tomorrow. She had no experience with the methods of agencies. No experience of how to convince strangers of her ability. But she had marked off three possible sources of jobs and after that, half a dozen apartments uptown. She pulled the covering sheet up to her chin and clutched it there. Life was changing. Faster, almost, than she could keep up with.

And still, the faces of Ralph and the lawyer she could not trust circled around each other, goading her.

When Sharon awoke the next morning, a dull throbbing had begun to pulse along the back of her neck. Her head felt like a box filled with restless animals trying to push up the lid. She sat up and waited to come clear of the vague dreams still webbing her thoughts. As she steadied herself against the loneliness that sifted through the webs of her imagination, she recalled scenes with Jay that had taken hold during sleep. Bands of aching muscles tried to restrict her enthusiasm to meet the coming challenges of job and apartment finding. She forced herself off the cot, hoping to leave behind the dreams of Jay.

From the medicine cabinet, she took four aspirin and gulped them down. She scowled at herself in the smeared mirror. *What the hell,* Sharon told herself, knowing that she had to accomplish these things; that she could never again return to her dependence on anyone else for protection. No one could get a new job for her, no one could give her peace of mind, no one could swaddle her away from the bruises of living. She had been a fool to believe in the simple, rosy path to home and family. A foolish hick who had gotten an education the hard way.

Sharon dressed slowly, handling her only pair of run-free stockings with delicate care. At least she had learned her lessons soon enough to try again. Her legs still looked good. Smooth and well-rounded in their sheer film of silk. And her belly still lay flat beneath the garter belt. Some man, somewhere, would want her again. Would love her and want to marry her. For a second, she closed her eyes and a cold shiver ran through her. Then Sharon laughed at herself, realizing the many good years of love still in her. She lifted her breasts into their bra cups, fondling each and recalling the touch of a man. Rapidly, she pulled her slip down to cover and protect her body from the thoughts flooding into her mind. Not now, when there was no man available to complete her desiring.

For breakfast, Sharon drank three cups of black coffee in a lively drugstore near Forty Second Street. She could sense the touch-and-go of the day's pulse as people around her gulped orange juice or bit into English muffins, then dashed on their way to something waiting.

Sharon had fifteen minutes still before her first appointment. She had come early on purpose to avoid the dishevelment of rushing and now she wandered up and down the aisles of the drugstore waiting for time to pass. She picked up and lay down rubber bath toys, cellophane bags of ball point pens. But her thoughts kept shouldering through these distractions, returning again and again to the problem of Leda and Ralph. *What if it's a trap? What if Leda stumbles right into…*

And finally it was nine o'clock. Sharon wrenched herself free of her thoughts and crossed through traffic. A narrow entrance-way brought her up a flight of winding steps and into the complications of form filling and waiting with the dozens of other girls to see one of the interviewers shadowed behind a row of translucent dividers.

The gloom of dull tans, the starkness of wooden chairs that reminded Sharon of high school, the restless, ill-concealed tension of other job seekers created an oppression that lay heavily on the new-grown bloom of her enthusiasm. Unfriendliness hung like droplets of mist to dampen with sleepiness and boredom all natural morning energies.

Instinctively, her mind snapped back to the fragrance of countryside. But then she pushed away the habit of Lynbrook, the mirage of happiness. For good or otherwise, city living had become her way. She had grown into the habit of crowds and complications. She had come to enjoy the stimulus to strive for something more, for progress, for possession, for change. Never again would she pine for the stodgy complacency, the vapid smugness of the old home town.

But even as Sharon fed herself these pills of encouragement, her thoughts kept snapping back to Leda. She seemed to be inside the woman's skin, living her life. What could she do to help Leda who had access, if she so desired, to the finest legal minds in the city?

All during the interview, Sharon had to keep forcing her mind back to the sprightly old maid fussing through a stack of cards. The job that Sharon had come for was gone. Taken the first thing Monday morning. Then why was the ad still in the paper? The woman shrugged and smiled helplessly. "Ad space," she said, which didn't explain anything to Sharon.

She waited while the woman thumbed through the file cards and called out possibilities. No, she had nothing else in the editorial field just now. Did Miss Porter know shorthand? No? Then how about something in the way of a receptionist. With only light switchboard duty.

Sharon left the office and ran down the steps like a rabbit miraculously freed from a trap.

An hour and a half of nothing. Would she find the same lack of response at the other agencies? This was, after all, the middle of the week.

She ran her comb quickly through the stray whisps of hair and continued cross-town. Considering the size of her bank balance, she just had to keep trying.

The second agency office had carpets on the floor and younger people at the desk. But the same tedious forms. The same request for job experience which looked desolately blank as she filled in her single employment line at Taft Publications.

The interviewer asked Sharon to explain what she had actually done in the way of magazine work.

And by two o'clock that afternoon, Sharon found herself in a labyrinth of littered rooms upstairs on Third Avenue, talking with the boss of a magazine that printed technical articles about furniture. The file cabinets and manuscripts and raincoats that hung from plastic hooks all smelled of cigar smoke. But Sharon could easily do the routine proof reading and seventy five dollars a week would keep her going till something better came up.

With heavy fingers, Sharon dialed the agency to acknowledge her new job and listened with dazed acceptance to the reminder that she pay the fee in three installments.

Sharon sat in the phone booth and tried to tell herself that she had already begun to accomplish something with her life. She remembered the waste baskets overflowing with crumpled paper, the gray window panes, the red return labels everywhere that screamed brashly *Melmac and Mahogany.* Her first job without anybody's help. It seemed to give a funny, brittle perspective to her life.

And then, as she thought of help, she thought once more of Leda and her mind began to spin with her own responsibility to this woman. Sharon dug out dimes and nickles, intent on finding Leda, intent on convincing her to get another attorney. Now that she was working things out for herself, she felt all the greater need to help her friend.

The phone rang and rang in her ear. Imaginatively, while she waited, Sharon told Leda that she had to fight Ralph, that she couldn't just give in to him. After all, Leda must have known that she herself had gone through hell to fight back at Jay. Her own example should have helped a little bit.

But no one answered the phone.

She took a cab to the three room apartment advertised for rent on East Ninety-Second Street. Cheap rent had lured her there. The narrow stone building was decorated with garbage cans. Some change from where she lived now, Sharon thought. But how do you find a nice place to live when you've just taken a fifty dollar cut in salary?

She unfolded the paper again and walked this time the seventeen blocks to the next address.

This time, the building looked clean on the outside. She had to go all the way up to the sixth floor apartment to find the nest of roaches swarming all over the oven.

And the next apartment had windows that pressed against the bricks of the building beside it.

"Plenty light enough," the superintendent said, pushing back his painter's cap from a white and green streaked forehead.

Sure, and plenty cool in August, Sharon thought as she smiled and said, "No, I don't think so."

Two hours and six apartments later, Sharon felt content as she paid a deposit on a furnished room in a clean hotel.

She lay down on the bed and pushed off her shoes. She could feel her feet expanding gratefully in their freedom. She sat up to rub her arches and looked around at the crisp white walls with black and white prints of the Parthenon and Acropolis. "Not bad," she said aloud in an effort to provide herself with company. At least she was paying by the week. If an apartment turned up, she could move in an instant.

Impulsively, she pushed a quarter into the coin operated radio and lay back again, yielding herself to the weight of preoccupations she could no longer evade.

So she had gotten a job and an apartment.

So she could be on her own, like any other adult.

So what?

Without thinking how smart or how stupid it was, she lifted the phone and said when Jay answered: "I need your help, Jay. I've got to find a good lawyer."

CHAPTER SIXTEEN

They had arranged to meet in a cafeteria near Jay's office.
As Sharon took a dinner check and scanned the warm, pink colored room for a secluded table, she remembered the years of quick lunches they had grabbed together. Good times, all in all, when you got right down to it. No real complications. Nothing so serious as the troubles that faced Leda. Her years with Jay had been—let's face it—innocent.

She changed a bill for nickles and carried a tray with four coups of coffee to a corner beneath the mosaic design of a mermaid that had so often brought obscene remarks into their conversation. The gold painted hands of a nautical clock jumped three minutes at a time. He would be prompt, of course. Too schedule conscious to keep her waiting. Both his fault and his virtue, she thought, now that she had no right to evaluate him at all.

For something to do, she began sipping at one of the cups, her glance darting away from and back to the revolving door each time it circled. When she saw him squeezing into the narrow partition, her fingers tightened around the hot porcelain, but she sat calm.

She watched him snap up the check and trim between the tables, moving rapidly, brusquely, with that no-nonsense style that could be so frightening, yet so reassuring, when you knew him. The navy blue tie hung still open from the office, his dark hair pushing forward along the arrow of his widow's peak. The whole pointed, masculine conception of him lashed toward her. Sharon felt the strength drain out of her arms.

"Thank you for coming," Sharon said on a dry throat.

He pulled out a chair and thrust himself down in an uncon-scious, wide movement of possesssion. "Now, what's all this about a lawyer?"

Sharon watched him pull forward one of the cups and dump in a stream of sugar. She hadn't expected him to be friendly. It was strictly one of those for-old-times agreements to help if he could.

"Can you sit through a complicated story?" she said, her words moving forward with caution.

"I'm here."

Sharon understood the abruptness and its implication of willingness. "The whole thing starts with me and my own par-ticular troubles, you might know." She smiled for a moment slyly. Then, holding the coffee cup between her palms, she began to describe the frustrations and the events which led, through Kermit, to her meeting with Leda and Ralph Michaels.

"I've heard of them," Jay said noncommittally.

"It seems everybody's heard of them. But no one really knows the truth. Not like I do," she murmured earnestly.

"All right, Miss Know-It-All, proceed."

And Sharon continued, speaking primarily to explain about Leda, but unable to separate Leda from an explanation of her own needs for growth and perspective. Speaking to Jay was not at all like talking to Mr. Donovan. Words tumbled from her, dis-secting coldly, almost cruelly the selfish advantage she had taken of Leda, explaining the lust for possession that had driven her into strange, untried paths of experience. Sharon spared noth-ing of her private anguish and humiliation, bringing out for Jay to see the night of her pick-up in the rain, the episode of child-hood relived in the shed with Eugene Kublick. But always, she returned to Leda. The woman's compliance and tenderness, the help she had been to Sharon when the woman's own world had crumbled to nothing.

"I owe it to her, Jay," Sharon concluded in a flush of passion. "I can't just sit by and let her destroy herself. That Donovan is a fake. I feel it in my bones that Ralph must have paid him off in some way. And the terrible thing is that Leda doesn't care any more." She waved away a cigarette. "She's given in to it because he's worn her out. And maybe she thinks it's right. Maybe she thinks it's her way of repenting, not to be able to see her kids ever again."

"And just how do you think you're going to change all this?" Jay said, spinning the tray of condiments on the table between them.

"I don't know, Jay. I don't know, but I've got to keep trying."

They sat for awhile now in an ebb of silence. Sharon felt herself scraping the bottom of her mind for other details that might help.

"There are a million lawyers in this city, Sharon. I don't see what that's got to do with convincing Leda to help herself."

But even as he spoke, Sharon detected a new twist of compliance. Encouraged, she leaned forward. "But you'll help me to convince her. You'll come along and speak to her with me?"

"What good would that do?"

"Well, how good can I be at this, all by myself? If you tell her, at least she'll listen. She knows about you. I've told her all about you. She'll listen."

Jay pushed his chair back. "Don't be so naive, Sharon. She's not about to listen to any strangers. Particularly not a man. Anyway," he took a stub of pencil from his jacket and scribbled something on a napkin, "here's the name of a pretty good guy. If you can convince her."

Sharon sat speechless as Jay shoved the paper at her and got up.

"Well, so long and good luck," he said.

Sharon waited till he had crossed the length of the room. She saw him pause at the counter to return the unclipped check. Then he pushed himself out onto the street and crossed between cars.

Sharon felt as though she had been dropped to the bottom of a dark well. And yet, what had she expected, violins and roses? From anyone else in the world, maybe. But not Jay Taft.

She lifted the limp napkin and folded it in half and in half again. Then she slid it behind the mirror in her bag. A long sigh of completion exhaled from her lungs. At least they were even now, she and Jay. He knew everything. All her actions. All her motives for the actions. And he must realize his own part in her decision to change her way of life. He could no longer believe that she had run out on him on a whim.

She stood up and gathered the remaining nickles from the tray. Her three years with Jay were now officially finished. She moved around a cart of dirty dishes and went downstairs to the line of phone booths. Maybe by now Leda would be at home.

Twice the receiver banged down in Sharon's ear and she knew that Ralph, at least, had come home.

But how would she get through to Leda? How, unless she went directly to the house? And if she did go to the house, how sure could she feel that Ralph could contain himself? Violence had always repelled her. And, more important, to mix in with Ralph now might undermine her value to Leda as a legal witness.

Yet she could not relax while she thought of Leda, alone with him. Her good sense gave way before the fears she felt for her friend.

Even in the cab heading for Leda's house, Sharon struggled to maintain the caution of good sense. She got out on Lexington Avenue and tried once more to phone.

Once more the receiver slammed down.

She had to go there. Had to face it with Leda. Protect Leda, if she could, by getting her out of that madhouse.

Sharon went up to the door and pressed firmly on the round black bell. Why hadn't she thought of all this yesterday? While there was still time? What had clogged her brains from inviting

Leda to stay with her? Was she still the selfish bitch who couldn't really think of anyone else's troubles?

She moved these thoughts away abruptly as she heard footsteps coming toward the door.

As the maid opened it, Sharon stepped quickly inside.

"Is Mrs. Michaels home?" she said, forcing her voice into pleasantry.

"Yes'm. I'll go tell her you're here." The maid waited now for Sharon to tell her name.

But she knew that it would be Ralph and not Leda who would come down. Holding her spine very straight, Sharon pressed forward into the huge livingroom, empty now of everything except the heavy furniture and the long shadows of ghosts.

"Tell her Miss Porter is here," Sharon said and clung to the arm of the chair into which she had lowered herself.

Hardly a minute later, Sharon knew that her final moment of quiet had passed for the day. She heard the sound of footsteps … how many of them? … clattering down the stairs, thudding angrily, sharply, even through the nap of the carpeting.

Leda and Ralph appeared at the same time. Ralph red-faced, hair sticking up, but very sober, cold and triumphant around the contemptuous slit of his mouth.

"You shouldn't have come," Leda said, the words as pale as her cheeks, as dull as the eyes that had sunk deeply into their bluish sockets.

"Don't worry, you'll get yours, too," Ralph said. "There's plenty to go around."

Sharon pushed herself up and started to move toward Leda. "Come with me out of here," she said in a whisper meant only for Leda.

But the words drifted across to Ralph and he stepped between them. "Go on, go with her. Feed the newspapers with your cheap, rotten scandal. I'll save the clippings for Tony to read when he learns the alphabet."

Sharon watched Leda's shoulders constrict as though a bullet had hit and lodged in her spine.

"Sharon, please go," she said.

"But you can't stay in this madhouse," Sharon insisted, reaching around Ralph to touch Leda's arm.

"Madhouse, is it?" Ralph shouted, his eyes widening. "You bitch, you whore. What do you know of madhouse? I'll smear you both from one end of the country to ..."

"Sharon, do as he says."

Sharon stepped back. Her nails dug into her clammy palms. "You can't give up, Leda. It was all my fault and everybody knows it. I can't let you suffer because of me. You've got to fight."

"Slut. For the last time ..."

Sharon leaned away from the thick, trembling hands that reached toward her shoulders. "Leda, please come. Please."

For answer, she saw Leda back away and start to go up the staircase.

"Leda," she called. "You can't ..."

But the woman did not even turn now to speak.

"You see," Ralph said. "It comes back home to all of us, doesn't it?"

The sight of his leering face with drops of perspiration sliding down from his sideburns made her dizzy. Her arm lashed out and swung in a ringing slap that made her arm sting up to the elbow.

Ralph's back arched. His mouth opened and searing, rocking laughter came from him. She could feel it stripping off Leda's skin, condemning the rest of her life to his control.

"It's not all finished yet," Sharon rasped, but her shoulders began to sag under the effort of courage. "You won't come out of this alive either."

She whirled and strode from the room, racing to get outside before the rising crest of misery inside her burst.

She ran across the street, jabbing at her eyes with the napkin on which Jay had written an address, feeling the hot flow of hopelessness release itself with bitter exhaustion. She paused and leaned against a store window, giving herself up to the wracking sobs that tore through her, uprooting all equilibrium. It was as though she had condemned Leda with her own two hands and there was no going back to try again. With her own selfishness, she had destroyed a life. The life of someone more needed in this world than herself. The life of someone with more brains and heart and charity.

"It didn't work out, did it?"

Sharon felt the grasp of strong fingers on her shoulder. She didn't have to look up. But in her hopelessness, she turned away from him. "You can't write this up for publication," she sobbed. "Why did you come around?"

"I don't know," his voice said honestly. "I guess maybe I wanted to be around. In case."

"Well, you missed all the fun," she said against the napkin. "Story's over."

"Then come on. I'll drive you back to your place."

Sharon felt too weak, too exhausted for argument. With docile steps, she followed Jay to the old blue Chevvy and sat beside him without speaking while he steered through traffic.

"I can't understand it," Sharon mumbled over and over. The horror of Leda's change trickled through her numbingly.

"Well, it wasn't your fault," Jay said, jumping a red light.

"But it was," Sharon said in a broken voice. "That's what I've been trying to tell you. The whole thing is all my fault, right from the beginning. I made her go away with me. She didn't want to go, Jay. I made her, do you hear? I begged her to go. I did. Myself." The words choked and dissolved into each other.

"What you need," Jay said evenly, "is a drink and a vacation from all this."

"I couldn't get drunk enough or run far enough to get that picture out of my mind." Sharon swallowed to steady herself. "Not ever."

"Well, let's try that drink anyway, okay?"

Sharon had no strength left to fight with him. Nor did she care to. After the mess she had made with Leda, she was willing for a while to let someone else call the tricks. Her big bid for independence was beginning to sound to her like a farce. If this was the best she could do for herself, she might as well stop trying. She deserved whatever she had coming to her. And especially from Jay.

They parked on a narrow street in the Village and Sharon let him steer her into the cozy odor of beer and pretzels.

He sat her down out of the light and ordered two double Scotches. "I don't blame you for not wanting to talk," he said. "But I hope you don't mind listening. There're a couple of things I'd like to say to you."

His voice filtered through to her as though from a great distance. She tried to concentrate, but her mind felt fuzzy and blurred.

"First of all," he began, "I didn't think you had that kind of guts. I don't mean to do the things you did. That sounded more like hysteria than anything else. And part of it, at least, was my own fault. But to come back here and face it all, girl. To face me, even. You kind of hit me below the belt in the cafeteria this afternoon, I have to admit. I didn't know anyone could get to be that honest."

Sharon turned from him and gazed without seeing out the door. She watched a guy trying to squeeze his convertible between two small cars. "It's not gonna fit," Sharon said as though talking across to him. Then she felt a hand on her arm, shaking her, jarring her.

"Listen to me, Sharon. Listen."

"I can't," she mumbled weakly. "I can't park the car."

Then she felt the world beginning to spin away, faster and faster, till it disappeared into darkness.

CHAPTER SEVENTEEN

Sharon awoke beneath a rough blanket that scratched at her eyelids. She lay quite still, sniffing at the sheets, listening intently for some clue to where she was.

Then, from the pillowcase she sensed the odor of a familiar hair tonic. How many times she had slept in this bed, without really belonging here. The pain of mixed memories began to wring through her. So it was beginning all over again. The whole bit had been in vain.

Sharon pushed herself up from the covers and contemplated with resignation the twin hair brushes that she'd bought him one Christmas, the red graph of circulation figures tacked with Scotch Tape beside a narrow mirror. The bedroom seemed rather dingy, gloomy, unlike what she might have remembered of Jay's bedroom. A ball of dust rolled across the bare floor to catch on the fringe of a runner.

How neglected and unhomelike, she thought listlessly.

She wanted to sit up, but a slow dizziness began the moment she came away from the pillow's support. Her legs and body felt oddly weak. She lay back again, panting.

But he was gone now. This was her chance to get dressed and get away. Gripping the mattress, she tried sitting up again. Her stomach began to lurch and she gave in to the need for rest.

On and off, she came awake, drifting to the surface like the stray planks of a sunken vessel.

She lay half between sleep and wakefulness when his key turned in the lock and she heard the crispness of paper bags rumple as he set them down on the table in the kitchen. She could tell by his footsteps as he moved about the apartment that he was trying to be quiet.

Sharon thought about calling him, but the effort seemed far too tremendous for her to make. While she listened to the sound of the refrigerator and cupboard doors opening to close again, she turned a little within the largeness of his pajamas. They folded over her feet and she caught the material between her toes in an habitual gesture that had always made her feel particularly feminine.

In a large swell of nostalgic feeling, she surfaced toward wakefulness.

She heard him creeping toward the room to peer in.

"Sharon?"

She couldn't move her arms but she managed to smile a little. She had the feeling that if she opened her mouth, her insides would heave up.

Jay went back into the kitchen and returned with a straight-backed chair.

She could see the yellow paint all nicked off. Used up carelessly like everything else in this apartment. Hardly a bachelor's lair, she thought. Hardly a place for seducing the kind of women she knew Jay liked.

Had she been wrong, too, in her evaluation of him? Her mind whirled with the strange possibility.

He turned the chair backward and straddled it so that they could look at each other without Sharon having to move her head.

Jay folded his arms across the top of the chairback and leaned his chin on his jacket sleeve. "I don't know what you're thinking inside that head of yours," he said gently. "Probably not too much right now, except how not to throw up. Am I right?"

Ever so slightly, Sharon nodded.

"So, as long as I've finally got you in a position where you can't talk back, you'll have to listen."

She felt a flutter of anger rising toward him from the fact that he knew so accurately how she felt. But the feeling returned to become part of the strange light-headed casualness she was experiencing.

"I've got only one thing to say," he went on, "and it's not a question. It's just this. I guess we've both grown up during this past week. And it's damned well time to quit kidding around and get started on those kids I'll be needing to take over the business."

Sharon closed her eyes, not wanting him to see the mixture of grief for Leda and wild happiness for herself rising madly to capture her. She wanted to reach out and touch him, let him know how she needed him. Had always needed him. She tried to lift a hand toward him. Beads of perspiration popped out on her forehead.

Jay got up from the chair and came to lean over her bed. "And furthermore," he said, blithely ignoring her discomfort, "don't be so foolish as to try to run away this time, because you won't get past the door."

Sharon did her best, but she couldn't muster even a smile. Why didn't he just stop yakking and hold her? Take away the butterflies buzzing in her stomach. She didn't need words. She needed ...

She managed the smile.

He put his lips to her forehead then and kissed her, very gently. "I'd do a hell of a lot better than this for you," he whispered against her skin, "only I'm sure you'd puke in my face."

Sharon's eyelids bounced open and she stared at him in mute but frantic question.

"Don't worry, honey," he said. "Isn't it just like you to get a virus in the middle of everything?"

Sharon sighed. As she felt his lips moving against her cheek, she began once more to sink away from consciousness. But she managed to grab his hand and hold on, knowing at last that Jay would be there still when she came awake.